Edward Stirling

Old Drury lane; fifty years' recollections of author, actor, and manager

Edward Stirling

Old Drury lane; fifty years' recollections of author, actor, and manager

ISBN/EAN: 9783741168062

Manufactured in Europe, USA, Canada, Australia, Japa

Cover: Foto ©Andreas Hilbeck / pixelio.de

Manufactured and distributed by brebook publishing software
(www.brebook.com)

Edward Stirling

Old Drury lane; fifty years' recollections of author, actor, and manager

OLD DRURY LANE.

OLD DRURY LANE

FIFTY YEARS' RECOLLECTIONS

OF

AUTHOR, ACTOR, AND MANAGER

BY

EDWARD STIRLING

IN TWO VOLUMES—VOL. II.

London

CHATTO AND WINDUS, PICCADILLY

1881

CONTENTS OF VOL. II.

BOOK III.

BOOK IV.

OLD DRURY LANE.

BOOK III.

ACTORS AND ACTRESSES WHO HAVE APPEARED AT
DRURY LANE THEATRE FROM ITS EARLIEST ANNALS
TO THE PRESENT TIME, SKETCHES OF THEIR CAREER,
AND ANECDOTES CONNECTED WITH THEM.

'Players are the abstracts and brief chronicles of the Time:
after your death, you were better have a bad epitaph than their
ill report.'

EDWARD KYNASTON, 1619—1687.

In the Restoration days (Charles II.), it was a frequent custom of the ladies of quality to carry Kynaston, the actor of Drury Lane and Lincoln's Inn Fields, in his female dress, after the performances, in their coaches to Hyde Park.

JOHN LACEY, 1622—1681.

John Lacey, a Yorkshireman and King's servant at Drury Lane, greatly relished by Charles II., who frequently commanded his performances.

CLUN (DIED 1664).

Tragic News, 1664.—'Clun, one of the best tragic actors at the King's House,

Drury Lane, last night going out of town, after he had acted the " Alchymist," to his country house, was set upon and murdered (one of the rogues taken, an Irish fellow) ; it seems most cruelly butchered and bound. The house (Drury Lane), will have a great miss of him.'—*Flying Post*, October 10th, 1664.   Clun acted the Lieutenant in the 'Humorous Lieutenant,' on the first night that Drury Lane opened.   He was a man of great talent, and universally respected.

THOMAS BETTERTON, 1635—1710.

BETTERTON preceded Garrick, and until that great actor's *début*, held the first rank on the boards of Drury.   His Hamlet, Romeo, Lear, Othello, suffered nothing by comparison with the same characters as played by our Roscius.   ' Silver-toned Betterton ' was a universal favourite.   He died in adverse circumstances, 1710.   Mrs. Barry and Mrs. Bracegirdle played in

' Love for Love,' at a benefit, to aid his slender means.

ELEANOR (NELL) GWYNNE, 1642—1691.

' Take care of poor Nell' were the last dying words that the merry monarch, Charles II., addressed to his brother, James Duke of York, at Whitehall. 'Nell,' the witty, lively incarnation of frolic and merriment, a welcome sight was her laughing face at all times to playgoers. She retained her popularity on and off the stage. Her first appearance at Drury Lane was in the 'Humorous Lieutenant,' as Cælia, and well she played the part. Pepys tells us he kissed her. Authors differ respecting Nell's birthplace ; but the 'Coal Yard,' Drury-lane, is believed to have been the place she first opened her merry eyes in.

> ' What needs a tongue to such a speaking eye,
> That more persuades than winning oratory.'

Hog-lane, Pipe-lane, Hereford, also claim pretty Nelly. Certain it is that she was buried, in 1691, in the church of St. Martin's-in-the-Fields. A dukedom emanated from the orange-girl of Lincoln's Inn Fields Theatre, and her connexion with Charles II., viz., that of St. Albans.

HART.

HART THE ACTOR, Drury Lane, had the reputation of being Nell Gwynne's first lover, and one of the hundreds of the Duchess of Cleveland's. Profligacy was the mode, equally practised by beggar and king, in the reign of Charles II.

GOODMAN.

PLAYER HIGHWAYMAN.—Goodman, of Drury Lane, famous in 'Alexander the Great,' a dashing impudent beau, styled 'Buck Goodman,' boasted of his exploits on the road. Whenever he wanted money the road furnished supplies. So well-to-do was he by his double calling, acting and stealing, that he once refused to play Alexander unless his duchess (Cleveland*) would be in the theatre to see him act.

WILLIAM MOUNTFORD, 1660—1692.

MOUNTFORD. — One of his Majesty's players, a great favourite with the ladies, both high-born and lowly.   He was handsome, well-bred, clever, and formed to please.   These enviable qualifications cost him his life.   He was murdered in Drury Lane, in 1692, by Captain Hill and Lord Mohun—rakes and mohawks, pests of society, a disgrace to a civilised country. Mrs. Bracegirdle was the *teterrima causa* of this cowardly midnight assassination. Hill fled the country: Mohun was tried for his life, but, through interest, escaped the gallows on which he so richly merited to swing.

* Goodman was one of the numberless paramours of this abandoned and lascivious woman.

SUSANNAH MOUNTFORD, 1669—1701.

MRS. MOUNTFORD, Colley Cibber said, was the mistress of more variety of humour than he had ever seen in any one actress. She came to Drury Lane with the united companies of Drury Lane and Dorset Gardens, Betterton and Mrs. Barry at the head. Mrs. Powell, Mrs. Verbruggen, Mrs. Bracegirdle, and last, but not least, Mrs. Jordan (not the celebrated comedy actress of a later time). Doggett, Morris, Mountford, were new comers. Mrs. Mountford was the most rakish and prettiest fellow on the stage in male attire —the ladies longing to enjoy what could never be theirs. She mimicked the beaux, fops, and bucks of the Restoration to the very life.

ANNE BRACEGIRDLE, 1663—1748.

ANNE BRACEGIRDLE.—This celebrated woman enjoyed a large share of patronage from all classes. She was exposed to evil report, simply because her private character was beyond reproach. Everybody was in love with Anne Bracegirdle. The town *(ton)* ran crazy after her: every beau and spark, juvenile, middle-aged or elderly, was mad to possess this beautiful woman. Mountford, as already related, died for her. She rejected the attentions of the great dramatist Congreve, who took his revenge by thus rather ungenerously be-rhyming her:

> ' Pious Belinda goes to prayers
>   Whene'er I ask the favour,
> Yet the tender fool's in tears
>   When she thinks I'd leave her.
> Would I were free from this restraint,
>   Or else had power to win her ;
> Would she could make of me a saint,
>   Or I of her a sinner.'

She lived respected to past fourscore years.

Congreve left £10,000 to Henrietta, Duchess of Marlborough. She spent

£7,000 of it on a diamond necklace, much to the envy of her high-bred friends.

Congreve deserted Mrs. Bracegirdle for the beautiful duchess. At her cost a monument was raised to his memory in Westminster Abbey.

BEN JOHNSON, 1665—1742.

BEN JOHNSON (not 'rare Ben'), a close copyist of nature. Wasp in 'Bartholomew Fair,' Morose in the 'Silent Woman,' were Teniers-like touches of art, worked out like his by attention to minutiæ in dress and colouring.

RICHARD ESTCOURT, 1668—1713.

ESTCOURT (author and actor), noticeable for his correct dressing and great care bestowed on everything that he attempted. Hamlet, Jaffier, Wildair, etc., all highly spoken of and commended.

COLLEY CIBBER, 1671—1757.

COLLEY CIBBER, manager of Drury,

a dramatic author and a sound good actor, rather inclined to ape the follies of the day in bedecking his person and endeavouring to lead the fashion. Lavishing his savings in the silly attempt, and forgetting the fable of the jackdaw, assuming peacock's feathers, he only drew on himself the ridicule of his fellow-comedians and the public.

BARTON BOOTH, 1681—1733.

BARTON BOOTH, a man of high birth, refined manners, and possessing no inconsiderable dramatic talents, reflected honour on the stage and Old Drury.

JOHN RICH, 1681—1761.

RICH, the renowned harlequin, the inventor of modern pantomime (borrowed from Italy), appeared for a season at Drury, which he quitted to become lessee of Covent Garden, making that theatre celebrated for its pantomimic performances.

ELIZABETH BARRY, 1682—1733.

MRS. BARRY, a first-class actress in tragedy, ruled the tragic throne until Sarah Siddons appeared to dispute it with her.

THOMAS DOGGETT (DIED 1721).

DOGGETT, whose loyalty to the Hanoverian rule displayed itself through the medium of a coat and silver badge to be rowed for annually on the king's birthday (1st August), by jolly young Thames watermen, was a first-class low comedian, and exceedingly popular with pit and gallery.

ANNE OLDFIELD, 1683—1730.

MRS. OLDFIELD, the daughter of a poor officer, was left to her own resources in early life. Beautiful, accomplished, surrounded by perils of pride allied to poverty, she was compelled to take a situation as barmaid in a tavern. Her beauty attracted a host of

admirers. To escape from their impor-
tunities, she quitted the ' bar ' for the stage,
at a very trifling salary—fifteen shillings
a week. Rich quickly saw her merit,
and engaged her for Drury Lane. Her
natural ability rapidly developed itself; in a
few months important characters were in-
trusted to her. Public favour followed, and
men of wealth and title became the pretty
barmaid's humble servants. This clever
woman lived to lead the fashions. Through
her refinement in taste she gave the fiat of
the mode; her natural inclination for display
and pride had here full scope.

After her death, Mrs. Oldfield lay in
state in the Jerusalem Chamber—House
of Lords—fashionably dressed in her coffin
with rich Brussels lace, headdress, double
lace ruffles, satin dress, and new kid gloves.
Pope writes thus of her:

' Let a charming chintz and Brussels lace
Wrap my cold limbs, and shade my lifeless face:

'One would not, sure, be frightful when one's dead;
And, Betty, give this cheek a little red.'

She was buried in Westminster Abbey.

JAMES QUIN, 1693—1766.

JAMES QUIN was born in Covent Garden, 1693, and educated in Dublin, where his father was a barrister. Quin appeared on the stage in Dublin, in little parts. After the season he came to London, first to Drury Lane, next to Lincoln's Inn Fields. By a casual appearance in 'Tamerlane' his great merit became known. In time he was proclaimed the first tragedian of the day. Garrick and Quin performed together in the 'Fair Penitent.' Quin retired in 1749. He instructed George III. in elocution. When the king delivered his first speech in Parliament, Quin was in the House of Lords to hear it. Much delighted, he exclaimed aloud: 'I taught the boy.'

QUIN AND THOMSON (author of 'The

Seasons ').—Quin heard that Thomson was confined in a spunging-house for a debt of seventy pounds ; he went to the house and was introduced to the poet. Thomson, much disconcerted at seeing Quin in such a place, as he had always taken pains to conceal his wants, Quin told him he was come to take supper with him, and that he had ordered it from an adjacent tavern ; half a dozen of claret was introduced. Supper over, and the bottle circulating, Quin said :

' It is time now we should balance accounts.'

This astonished poor Thomson, who began to think Quin had some demand upon him. Our actor, smiling, continued :—

' Mr. Thomson, the pleasure I have had in reading your works, I cannot estimate at less than a hundred pounds—no words ; I insist upon paying my debt ;'—putting down a hundred-pound note, and hastily taking his leave before Thomson could reply.

DRURY LANE, 1748.—Rich, manager; Quin, actor. Quin retired in a fit of spleen to Bath in order to injure Rich, he being then engaged at Drury Lane. After a few days Quin relented for having used Rich so ill, and wrote to him in this laconic fashion :

> ' I am at Bath.
>
> > ' QUIN.'

The manager's reply was both laconic and defiant :

> ' Stay there and be d——d.
>
> > ' RICH.'

The day before Quin died he drank a bottle of claret. Being sensible of his approaching end, he said he could wish that the last tragic scene was over, though he was in hope he should be able to go through it with becoming dignity. He died at Bath in 1766, aged 73.

'THE FATAL RETIREMENT' (tragedy),
A. Brown, Drury Lane, 1714.—This play
would not be worth notice, were it not for
an event connected with it.

When it was offered to the manager.
Quin, he refused to act in it, and to this
circumstance the author's friends attributed
its failure. They repeatedly insulted Quin
for several nights during his performances.
He at last appealed to the audience, informing them that he had, at the request of the
author, read his piece before it was acted,
and given his sincere opinion of it : viz.,
that it was the very worst play he had ever
read in his life, and for that reason he
refused to act in it. This explanation
turned the tide in Quin's favour ; instead
of hisses, applause greeted the actor ever
after.

MRS. PRITCHARD, 1711—1768.

MRS. PRITCHARD (born 1711), with many
disadvantages of a neglected education, by

conduct and persevering industry, raised
herself to the highest rank in her calling,
sustaining the leading female characters in
Garrick's performances with credit to herself, and with the approval of her manager.
'Little David' was very chary with his
praise, but to Mrs. Pritchard he never
spared it, a convincing proof of her excellence and worth.

KITTY CLIVE (born 1711) first played a
boy's part in a play entitled 'Mithridates ;'
salary twenty shillings per week. Her
beautiful face and figure delighted the
town. She became a popular toast at
Clubs, and a subject for the tittle-tattle of
coffee-houses. Not to have seen sweet
Kitty Clive, was considered equivalent to
being 'out of the world.' She retained
her influence to the last. She was the
daughter of William Rastor, an Irish
gentleman ; but the fortunes of the family

having sunk to a low ebb, we find her engaged as a servant of all work, living at the house of a Mr. Snell, a fan-painter in Church-row, Houndsditch. Watson, a box-keeper at Drury Lane, kept the 'Bell tavern, opposite Snell's. At this house was held the 'Beef-steak' Club. Kitty Rastor was washing the doorsteps one day, and singing merrily, with the club-room windows open. They were speedily crowded by the members, enchanted by her natural grace and simplicity. This circumstance led her to the stage, under the patronage of Mr. Beard and Dunstall, both connected with Drury Lane. Her first appearance was in the year 1728 at Drury Lane. Her second character was Phillida in Cibber's 'Love is a Riddle.' The enemies of the author, determined to condemn the comedy without a hearing, assembled in great numbers for that purpose. When Kitty Clive appeared, applause drowned the hisses. One

of the rioters in a stage-box called out :
' Zounds, Tom, take care ; the charming
little devil will save all.'   Her performance
of Nell in ' The Devil to Pay' (1731)
fixed her reputation in that species of
character.   In 1732 she married George
Clive, a lawyer, brother of Baron Clive.
The union proved unhappy, and a separation soon took place.   In 1740 she was
selected to act ' Alfred,' played at Chesden
House, before the Prince of Wales.   When
she retired from the stage, Garrick vainly
tried to persuade her to act longer ; her
reply was a positive ' No.'   He asked her
how much she was worth ?   She answered,
as much as himself.   He smiled at her supposed misunderstanding of his meaning.

' No, no,' she said, ' I know when I've
enough ; you never will.'

On the 24th of April, 1769, the comedy
of the ' Wonder ' and ' Lethe ' were acted

for Mrs. Clive's benefit; and on that evening she took leave of the stage in an epilogue, written by Horace Walpole, the concluding lines of which were :

> ' I will not die, let no vain panic seize you ;
> If I repent, I'll come again and please you.'

Garrick asked her opinion of the acting of Mrs. Siddons. She replied, that ' it was all truth and daylight.' The following is Churchill's character of Kitty Clive :

> ' First giggling, plotting chambermaids arrive,
> Hoydens and romps, led on by General Clive.
> In spite of outward blemishes, she shone,
> For humour famed, and humour all her own ;
> Easy, as if at home, the stage she trod,
> Nor sought the critic's praise nor fear'd his rod.
> Original in spirit and in ease,
> She pleased by hiding all attempts to please,
> No comic actress ever yet could raise
> On Humour's base more merit or more praise.'

Mrs. Clive died December 6th, 1785. Her conduct in private life was not only laudable, but exemplary.

TASWELL (prompter, Drury Lane) and

Mrs. Clive disputing together, both greatly excited, high words arose. Taswell ended the fray by saying, 'Madam, I have heard of tartar and brimstone; but, by G—, you are the cream of one, and flower of the other.'

DAVID GARRICK, 1716—1779.

. DAVID GARRICK was the grandson of a French merchant, who settled in England on the Revocation of the Edict of Nantes by Louis XIV. Garrick's father, a captain in the army, being on a recruiting party at Hereford, his son was born at an inn there, in the early part of the year 1716; educated at Lichfield, and afterwards placed under the care of Samuel Johnson, with whom he came to London in 1735.

Garrick embarked in the wine trade; this not suiting his inclination, he turned his thoughts to the stage, and in 1741 made his appearance, under the name of

'Lyddal' at Ipswich, in the character of Aboan in 'Oroonoko.' On the 19th of October in the same year, he came out in 'Richard the Third,' at the theatre in Goodman's Fields,* and here his popu-

* The following is a copy of the original bill of Garrick's first appearance in London, October 19th, 1741, at the theatre in Goodman's Fields:

'This day will be performed a concert of vocal and instrumental music, divided into parts. Tickets at three, two, and one shilling. Places for the boxes to be taken at the 'Fleece' tavern, next the theatre.

'N.B. Between the acts of the concert will be presented an historical play, called

'"THE LIFE AND DEATH OF RICHARD THE THIRD,"

containing the distress of King Henry VI., the artful acquisition of the crown by Richard, the murder of the young King Edward V. and his brother in the Tower, the landing of the Earl of Richmond, and the death of King Richard in the memorable battle of Bosworth Field, being the last that was fought between the Houses of York and Lancaster, with many true historical passages.

'The part of King Richard by a gentleman who never appeared on any stage.

'KING HENRY, *Mr. Giffard.*
EARL OF RICHMOND, *Mr. Marshall.*

larity exceeded all that had ever been known in dramatic history. The other houses were deserted, which so provoked the patentees, that they exerted their interest in getting the rival theatre sup-

PRINCE EDWARD, *Miss Hippisley.*
DUKE OF YORK, *Miss Naylor.*
DUKE OF BUCKINGHAM, *Mr. Paterson.*
DUKE OF NORFOLK, *Mr. Blake.*
LORD STANLEY, *Mr. Pagett.*
EARL OF OXFORD, *Mr. Vaughan.*
TRESSEL, *Mr. W. Giffard.*
CATESBY, *Mr. Neame.*
RATCLIFFE, *Mr. Croft.* ·
TYRELL, *Mr. W. Giffard.*
LORD MAYOR, *Mr. Dunstable.*
THE QUEEN, *Mrs. Steel.*
DUCHESS OF YORK, *Mrs. Yates.*

And the part of Lady Anne by Miss Giffard. With entertainment of dancing, by Monsieur Froune, Madame Duvalt, and the two Masters and Miss Grainers.

   ‘ To which will be added a Ballad Opera in one act, called

   ‘ “THE VIRGIN UNMASKED,”

(the part of Lucy by Miss Hippisley) ; both of which will be performed gratis by persons for their diversion.

   ‘ The Concert will begin exactly at six o’clock.’

pressed. Garrick now entered into a contract with Fleetwood of Drury Lane, and in the ensuing summer was invited to Dublin, where the concourse of spectators was so great every night as to occasion a disorder, which went by the name of 'Garrick's Fever.' He became a joint partner in Drury Lane with Lacy in 1747, and married Mdlle. Violetta, a Viennese *danseuse.* On the death of Lacy in 1773, he became sole manager of the theatre, which he sold for £35,000 to Sheridan, Linley, and Ford.

Garrick's last appearance on the stage was at Drury Lane, June 10th, 1776, as Don Felix in the comedy of the 'Wonder.' He died January 20th, 1779, and was buried in Westminster Abbey. He wrote innumerable dramatic pieces, songs, prologues, epilogues, etc.

Garrick's farewell address, Drury Lane, June 10th, 1776 :

' LADIES AND GENTLEMEN,

' It has been customary with persons under my circumstances to address you in a farewell epilogue. I had the intention, and turned my thoughts that way; but indeed I found myself *then* as incapable of writing such an epilogue, as I should be *now* of speaking it: the jingle of rhyme and the language of fiction would but ill suit my present feelings. This is to me a very awful moment; it is no less than parting for ever with those from whom I have received the greatest kindness and favours, and upon the spot where that kindness and those favours were enjoyed—' (*he was unable to proceed until relieved by tears*).

' Whatever may be the changes of my future life, the deepest impression of your kindness will always remain here' (*his hand on his breast*) 'fixed and unalterable.

'I will very readily agree to my successors having more skill and ability for their station than I have ; but I defy them all to take more sincere and more uninterrupted pains for your favour, or to be more truly sensible of it, than is your humble servant.'*

GARRICK, 1771.—The Empress Catherine offered, through her minister, two thousand guineas to Garrick for four performances at St. Petersburg. Of course this offer was refused.

GARRICK, greatly annoyed by ladies of quality who frequented the boxes continually talking louder than the players, determined to give one of the chief offenders, Lady Coventry, a delicate hint on the subject. Speaking an epilogue, he glanced towards her ladyship's box :

> 'May I approach unto the boxes, pray,
> And there search out a Judgment on the play ?
> In vain, alas ! I should attempt to find
> Fine ladies *see* a play, but never *mind it.*'

* See Davies's Life of Garrick (Lond., 1780), ii. 328-9.

Lady Coventry one night was so noisy, and laughed so loud, while Mrs. Bellamy was performing in the character of Juliet, and repeating her soliloquy previous to taking Friar Lawrence's potion, that the actress was unable to go on, and left the stage in tears. The audience would not suffer the play to proceed until Lady Coventry and her party had quitted the theatre.

GARRICK'S SCORE at the Crown Hotel, Bow-street :—Sundry glasses of punch for Don Felix ; glasses of brandy for Richard and Macbeth ; stout, Lear's drink ; love-stricken Romeo drank claret—total, 7s. 6d. Little David studied economy in his drinks as in other things. This bill was paid by Topham the treasurer, and entered in the accounts of Old Drury.

MRS. MACAULAY.—When Mrs. Macaulay published her book, 'Loose Thoughts,' Garrick was asked if he did not think it a strange title for a lady to choose. ' By no means,' replied he ; ' the sooner a woman gets rid of such thoughts the better.'

GARRICK AND STONE.—Garrick always employed Stone to procure auxiliaries for him at Drury Lane. He was what we now call a 'super-master.' This man was nick-named 'the theatrical Crimp.' A variety of letters passed between Garrick and Stone. The following was written in 1748 :

'SIR MR. GARRICK,

'Mr. Lacy* turned me out of the lobby and behaved very ill to me. I only axed for my two Guineas for the last Bishop —and he swore I should not have a farthing. I can't live upon nothing. I have a couple of cupids, you may have cheap—as they belong to a poor journeyman shoemaker who I drink with,—I am your humble servant,

'Wm. STONE.'

* Garrick's partner.

Garrick's reply was as follows :

'STONE, you are the best fellow in the world.   Bring the cupids to the Theatre to-morrow.   If they are under Six, and well made, you shall have a guinea a-piece for them.   Mr. Lacy will pay you himself for the Bishop.   He is very penitent for what he has done.   So you can get me two good murderers, I will pay you hand-somely, particularly the spouting fellow who keeps the apple-stall on Tower-Hill, the cut in his face is quite the thing.   Pick me up an Alderman or two for Richard, if you can ; The Barber will not do for Brutus, although I think he will succeed in Mat.

'DAVID GARRICK.'

The following will explain themselves :

'SIR,

'The Bishop of Winchester is getting drunk at the Bear and swears —— his eyes if he'll play with you to-night,

'I am yours, W. STONE.'

Reply ;

 ' STONE,

  ' The Bishop may go to the devil.
I do not know a greater rascal except
yourself.

    ' D. GARRICK.'

GARRICK AND THE AMATEUR.—A young
gentleman, introduced by a nobleman,
obtained a hearing from Garrick much
against his will.

' Well, sir, you wish to become an actor,
Lord N—— tells me ?'

' ASPIRANT *(mildly)* : ' Yes, sir.'

' What have you studied ?'

' Hamlet,' the reply.

' Give me a taste of your quality—a
speech.'

With vast pomposity the youth commenced : ' To be—or not to be ?'

' Stop, stop, sir !' cried Garrick—' not to
be, by G—d !' and rushing out of the room,
he left the astonished tragedian to himself.

SAMUEL FOOTE, 1721—1777.

SAMUEL FOOTE, dramatist, actor and satirist.—Talent and selfishness were oddly blended in Foote's character. On all occasions he strove to crush his brother performers on the stage. Foote's solo entertainments were given at the Haymarket, He originated this form of amusement—a narrative, interspersed with imitations, songs and *on dits* of the passing hour. This novelty told well with the town, and brought Foote money and fame. His comedies contain much originality and natural description of character. Mrs. Cole stands yet without a rival.

FOOTE possessing unlimited convivial talent, had recourse to it for support. His powers of ridicule, buffoonery and satire led him to give an entertainment at the Haymarket. Having no dramatic licence, he called it 'Tea in a Morning.' The

Duke of York procured a patent for him, being partial to his company.

A Duke of Norfolk, an inveterate worshipper of the jolly god Bacchus, wishing to make a novel appearance at a masquerade, consulted Foote what new character he should go in. 'Go sober,' replied the satirist, 'that will be a novelty.'

MRS. FOOTE (mother of Sam. Foote), nearly as eccentric and improvident as her clever son, wrote to him, a prisoner for debt:

> 'DEAR SAM,—I'm in prison.
> 'ANNE FOOTE.'

Foote replied :

> 'DEAR MOTHER,—So am I.
> 'SAM FOOTE.'

GARRICK'S BUST.—A gentleman calling on Foote took notice of a bust of Garrick on a bureau :

'Do you know my reason,' says Foote 'for making Garrick stand sentry there ?'

' No,' replied his friend.

' I placed him there,' resumed the wit, 'to take care of my money ; for in truth I can't take care of it myself.'

Foote was a notorious spendthrift ; whereas Garrick was remarkable for a thrift verging on penuriousness.

FOOTE, RICH, AND TATE WILKINSON.

RICH, manager of Covent Garden, lacked education, but was a genius in pantomime. Foote's ' Minor ' being fixed for immediate representation, Rich asked Wilkinson to cast the piece, because he did not understand anything about ' Mr. Footsey's' farce.' Foote hearing of this arrangement, rushed in one morning, astonishing Rich, Sparks, and Wilkinson sitting in council.

' You old scoundrel' (*to Rich*), ' if you dare let that pug-nosed fellow' (Wilkinson) 'take any liberty with my piece, I'll bring you on the stage. If you want to engage that pug, black his face, and let him hand the tea-kettle in one of your stupid pantomimes. But if he dares to appear in any character in the " Minor," I will instantly show up your old, silly, ridiculous self with your three tomcats and your pug-dog' *(pointing to Wilkinson)* 'all together, next week, at Drury Lane. I will exhibit you in the pantomime for the pit and gallery to laugh at. That will be paying you a great compliment, you squinting old Hecate!'

RICH: 'Oh dear me, Muster William-shun, if I lets you act Footsey'll bring me and my cats on the stage, at Dreary Lane. Oh dearee me, what a man he is !'

Tate Wilkinson relates this anecdote in his Diary.

PEG WOFFINGTON, 1718—1760.

PEG WOFFINGTON (born 1718) was the incarnation of merriment : more piquant sayings and *bons mots* are recorded of her than of any actress before or since. She was an immense favourite in her native city of Dublin, for her lovely person and her perpetual flow of gaiety. She appeared at Drury Lane in 1738, and at once secured a leading position. Her Sir Harry Wildair eclipsed all her previous efforts. A brilliant career in comedy (and sometimes tragedy) attended her, until she quitted her busy scene of mimic life for retirement, in 1757.

EDWARD SHUTER, 1728—1776.

SHUTER, the great comedian, in the early part of his life was a pot-boy at a public-house, near Covent Garden. A gentleman one day ordered him to call a hackney-coach. It so happened the gentleman left his gold-headed cane in the coach, and, missing it next morning, went immediately to the public-house to inquire of the boy Ned who called the coach, whether he could tell him the number. Shuter was then no great adept in figures, except in his own way of scoring up a reckoning : '44, for two pots of porter; o, for a shilling's worth of punch and a paper of tobacco.' The gentleman, upon this, was as much at a loss as ever, till Ned whipped out a piece of chalk and thus scored the reckoning : 44, for two pots of porter; o, for a shilling's worth of punch, and a line across the two pots of porter for a paper of tobacco, forming the numbers 440. The gentleman recovered his cane, and thinking it a pity such acuteness should be buried in an ale-house, took him away and put him to school, thereby enabling him to become the first comedian of his time.

Epitaph on Ned Shuter (Drury Lane).

> ' Below in bed
>   Lies honest Ned,
> Who harm ne'er did nor meant ;
>   Who had no spice
>   Of heinous vice,
> So little to repent.
>   With heart sincere,
>   And friendly ear
> He freely dealt his pelf ;
>   In life like this,
>   Whate'er's amiss,
> Correct it in thyself.'

THOMAS WESTON, 1727—1776.

Weston at first appeared at Drury Lane as a substitute for Shuter. On one occasion, Shuter's name being in the bills and Weston playing the part, loud cries of 'Shuter' were raised when he entered, from Pit and Galleries. Mrs. Clive was acting Kitty Pry. Nothing could be heard but '*Shuter!*' Weston, in seeming stupid amazement, pointed to Mrs. Clive :

' Why should I *shoot her?* Surely she plays her part well enough.'

This settled the storm. Rounds of applause followed.

JOHN MOODY, 1728—1813.

MOODY, known in theatrical circles as 'the Irish Gentleman,' was the original Major O'Flaherty. A native of Cork, he invariably denied his connexion with Ireland. His Teague was inimitable, and as Sir Callaghan O'Brallaghan in ' Love-à-la Mode,' Sir Patrick O'Neal in the ' Irish Widow,' he was superior to all rivals.

DAVID ROSS (BORN 1728).

Ross, 1751, first played at Drury Lane secondary characters in tragedy, leading in comedy. He opened a new theatre in Edinburgh ; the first patent was given to Ross. It was to this player that a sum of ten guineas was sent anonymously every year on his benefit for his acting of ' George Barnwell,' the guilty apprentice, by some repentant sinner. Ross lost his earnings in the Edinburgh venture. He returned to London with impaired fortunes, and re-appeared at Covent Garden ; but he had lost his attractive powers.

HENRY MOSSOP, 1729—1773.

This excellent actor came from Ireland, a land so prolific in miracles, handsome women, and clever men. He was a native of Dublin. After enjoying popularity for a time, fortune deserted him, and he died poor, and in obscurity.

THOMAS KING, 1730—1805.

KING ('Gentleman King'), high-life comedian, played men of fashion, fops, and eccentric characters, in a consummate and masterly style. Lord Foppington, Charles Surface (original), Copper, Captain Flutter, etc., were personations perfected by King's gentility and accomplishments. Courted by the best circles, King lived and died a gentleman, and an ornament of the profession that he loved so well.

MRS. ABINGTON, 1731—1815.

MRS. ABINGTON (born 1731), one of the best of English comedy actresses: her ‘Mrs. Pine’ has been immortalised by the pencil of Sir Joshua Reynolds, whose portrait gives us a fair notion of this attractive woman's features. Her never-tiring animal spirits contributed largely to her popularity.

GEORGE ANN BELLAMY, 1733 (?)—1788

GEORGE ANN BELLAMY was a finished actress and a lovely woman—good ingredients these for public favour at all times—much envied by her famous rival in male attire, Peg Woffington. These two celebrities ran a race for Thespian supremacy. Critics and impartial judges were puzzled which to choose, and so wisely chose both.

ROBERT BADDELEY, 1732—1794.

ROBERT BADDELEY, donor of Old Drury's Twelfth Cake. — An excellent actor, especially in his personations of old men in comedies. To his care and benevolent feeling we are indebted for an original idea, establishing a home for actors and actresses. This gave the notion of a fund at the Patent House (now so rich), 1793. A sum in the consols, left by Baddeley, gives the annual Twelfth Cake to the comedians of Drury Lane; this added to another, with sundry bowls of punch (the gift of the manager), gladdens the hearts of her Majesty's servants yearly.

BADDELEY, previous to his trying the stage, held an ensign's commission in a marching regiment. Ensign's pay at that time did not run to luxuries, so he quitted the military for the more congenial and lucrative theatrical profession. Braddeley rapidly rose to a first-rate position in his new calling, receiving a good salary for those days, fifteen pounds a week. Meeting two of his brother officers in the Strand,

they strove to pass by our actor without re-
cognition. This would not do for Baddeley:
he accosted them heartily. Inquiries were
exchanged. One of them asked Baddeley
what he got by his acting ?

'From twelve to fifteen pounds a week.'

'Gude save us ! what, mon ?' exclaimed a
Scotch officer. 'Fifteen puns in siller ? ye
dinna mean to fash me ?'

'No, it's the plain truth,' laughingly
replied our Drury Lane actor.

Astonished Caledonian : 'Ma Gud ! ha'
ye ony vacancies in your corps ? I'll sell
out, and list on the stage to-morrow.
Gude save us I Fifteen puns !'

At the close of Drury Lane seasons,
Baddeley gave solo entertainments at
Marylebone Gardens. The following is a
copy of one of the advertisements :

'At Marylebone Gardens, to-morrow the
30th, will be presented

'"THE MODERN MAGIC LANTERN,"

in three parts, being an attempt at a sketch of the times in a variety of characters, accompanied with a whimsical and satirical dissertation on each character by R. Baddeley, comedian.

'Bill of Fare.—Part First: A Modern Patriot; a Serjeant-at-Law; a Duelling Apothecary; Andrew Marvell; Lady Fribble and Foreign Quaker; a Widow.

'Part Second: A Man of consequence; Lady Tit-for-Tat; a Hackney Parson; an Italian Tooth-drawer; a Maccaroni Parson; a Hair-dresser; High Life in St. Giles's; a Jockey; a Robin-hood Orator; a Jew's Catechism.

'Part Third will consist of a short sketch, "PUNCH'S ELECTION."

'Admittance, two shillings and sixpence each, coffee or tea included. The doors to be opened at seven, and the exordium to be spoken at eight o'clock.

'*Vivant Rex et Regina!*

' N.B.—The Gardens will be opened on Sunday evenings for company to walk.'—*Morning Chronicle* and *London Advertiser*, May 29th, 1775.

WILLIAM POWELL, 1736—1769

POWELL, a favourite actor at Old Drury Lane, playing Lothair in the ' Fair Penitent,' in the last scene, a dead man (supposed to be Lothair's body) lies covered on a bier in Calista's funeral chamber. Powell's dresser Warren, not displeased at the chance of earning a shilling, took Lothair's place on the bier ; this was unknown to his master (rather quick-tempered). Powell, missing his dresser, called loudly for him, ' Where's that rascal Warren ?' ' Where, sir ?— dead,' cries the affrighted dresser from the bier, to the horror of Calista. Warren's delay roused Powell's passion to fever-heat, and he bawled threats that every bone in the unfortunate dresser's skin should be broken. Warren jumped up in his shroud, with all the sombre trappings around him ; unfortunately he was tied to the bier. Roars of laughter greeted the poor fellow's return to life. Making a desperate effort to run, dragging the bier along with him, he knocked the fair Calista down, and made his escape. The play ended with jests and jibes, at the cost of the ' Fair Penitent.'

TATE WILKINSON, 1736—1803.

TATE WILKINSON (York Circuit manager), patronised by Garrick, and engaged at Drury Lane—never an actor, always a mimic. He was manager of the first Circuit in England. His mimicry of ' Actors of the Old School' was a reproduction of their voice and manner, as they lived.

Theatres, under Wilkinson's government, produced and perfected more actors of eminence for the London theatres than any other.

WILLIAM PARSONS, 1736—1795.

PARSONS, a capital actor in representations of old men. Among many original parts that fell to his lot during a long career of thirty-seven years—Crabtree, Sir Fretful Plagiary, Sir Christopher, Curry, Snarl, etc. His racy humour acted like a spell upon his auditors. Yells of laughter were provoked by his funny looks. He amassed and left considerable wealth, which, however, was quickly dissipated by his widow, a *quondam* Miss Stewart, niece to the Earl of Galloway.

MRS. YATES (1737—1787).
MRS. POPE (1740—1797).

MRS. YATES, MRS. POPE.—These ladies both possessed abilities of a high order. The latter was an especial favourite of Garrick—no small praise.

WILLIAM BENSLEY, 1738—1817.

BENSLEY (once an officer in the army) first appeared at Drury Lane in 1765, as Pierre in ' Venice Preserved.' His Ghost in ' Hamlet,' Malvolio in ' Twelfth Night,' Iago, etc., were considered performances of high merit.

LEE LEWES, 1740—1803.

LEE LEWES, equally appreciated either in Harlequin or Foppington ; but our critical forefathers failed in their appreciation of his self-estimated abilities. His conceit amounted to the sublime.

JAMES DODD, 1741—1796.

DODD, the prince of fops, the pink of taste, with his clouded canes, his powdered periwigs, his enamelled snuff-boxes and pretty oaths—' 'Fore Gad !' 'Stap my vitals !' ' Yoicks !' etc. Dodd, a master of all the frivolities, imitating to the life the movements, appearance, sayings, and doings of the men of fashion and ton in 'Lord Foppington,' reproduced at Old Drury.

ANNE CATLEY, 1745—1789.

ANNE ('NAN') CATLEY—of lowly origin ; her early career was beset with privations and difficulties which she overcame by a strong will and ready wit. Resolved to succeed, she did. Full of life, spirit, and vivacity, 'Nan' worked her way to Old Drury.

> 'A merry heart goes all the day,
> Your sad one tires in a mile-a.'

Catley became a town toast—her assurance surpassed all others. After some years of indulgence in promiscuous amours, which rather scandalised the proprieties, she married General Lascelles, and quitted her mimic scenes for the realities of domestic life

JOHN HENDERSON, 1747—1785.

HENDERSON, a leading tragedian, had a fine voice and person. He held a distinguished place in the histrionic world for many years. His Macbeth, Lear, and Coriolanus met with great and deserved praise at Drury Lane.

JOHN PALMER, 1747—1798.

JOHN PALMER, versatile and clever.— Nothing came amiss to Palmer : Shylock or Falstaff, Mercutio, Abel Drugger or Jerry Sneak !

JOHN QUICK, 1748—1831.

QUICK, one of the vainest men of his day, enjoyed the favour and patronage of King George III. He gave himself most ridiculous airs. Vain by nature, his folly increased tenfold with age. He tried tragedy after Garrick's style (it proved to be a long way *after* it), and failing, turned to comedy, in which he speedily rose in public estimation, made money, and died.

Quick, in his early strolling-days, often played in two or three pieces nightly, for one shilling ; on one occasion his shilling's-worth was Richard the Third, and Sharp in the ' Lying Valet '—a cheap shilling's-worth.

JOHN EDWIN, 1750—1790.

EDWIN, after having failed at Drury Lane, ultimately became popular, more especially in O'Keefe's operas : his singing was excellent and highly appreciated.

JACK JOHNSTONE, 1750—1828.

JACK JOHNSTONE, a son of the Emerald Isle.—No better representative of the Irish character ever trod the stage. His spirit, by nature rollicking and full of gaiety, out-did itself when portraying the ' broths of boys' from Connaught, Tipperary, or Cork. Dublin Jackeens gained an addition

of wit and oddity from Jack's vein.   His
singing was capital, and was always encored.
He fortunately lived at a period when real
comedies were written and listened to.
The original parts that fell to Johnstone's
lot were numerous ; old Drury's walls rang
with merriment, arising from this clever
comedian's aptitude to please.   ' A boy for
bewitching them,' ripe and ready for a fight
or frolic, was Jack.   The audiences fre-
quenting Drury Lane greatly patronised
this '*nale* Irishman's' acting.   He had (as
I already said), the singular good fortune to
live when comedy was popular, and the
writers of comedy clever and practical,
emerging from coarse ribaldry and obscene
jests, insulting to sense and morality.   The
laxity of such writers as Congreve, Farquhar, and Wycherley had subsided into
a better tone, raising the drama in social
estimation.   At length Johnstone retired
from the stage to enjoy his well-won

savings.   He was born in 1750, and died in 1828.

SAMUEL REDDISH (DIED 1785).

SAMUEL REDDISH, an Irish actor, appeared first in Smock Alley Theatre, Dublin, 1763.   Reddish came to Drury Lane in 1767, appearing as Lord Townley in 'The Provoked Husband': Lady Townley, Mrs. Abington.   Indulging in high life and its excesses, his brilliant career was brief; on one occasion he apologised for his incapability of utterance caused by too great indulgence in wine.   His second wife, Mrs. Canning, was mother of George Canning, Prime Minister of England.

MRS. CANNING.

MRS. CANNING appeared first at Drury Lane in 1773, in the character of Jane Shore, and held a good position with the public.   Her second husband, Reddish, gradually lost his memory; his mind became diseased, and he died in a lunatic asylum at York.

SARAH SIDDONS, 1755—1831.

SARAH SIDDONS was born at Brecon in Wales, in 1755, in a public-house, ‘The Shoulder of Mutton,’ situated in the centre of the town, and much frequented by the inhabitants. Her father, Roger Kemble,* was always a welcome guest at their jolly meetings. Kemble was a man of respectable family, and possessed a small property in Herefordshire. Marrying the daughter of a provincial manager, he received a company of strolling players for her dowry, and set up as manager for himself. Mr.

---

* Roger Kemble, father of the talented Kemble family, John, Stephen, Charles, and Sarah (Mrs. Siddons), died December 6, 1802, aged eighty-two years. His name will ever remain memorable in theatrical history; his children's talents having shed such a lustre on the English stage. Mr. Kemble, although comparatively a poor man, gave all his children an excellent education.

Ward, his father-in-law, disapproved of his daughter's marrying an actor, and when he found that she had secretly married Roger Kemble, he refused to see her. After a time he was with difficulty persuaded to speak to her, and to accord her his forgiveness, with all the bitterness of his heart saying :

'Sarah, you have not disobeyed me; I told you never to marry an actor, and you have married a man who neither is nor ever can be one.'

The whirligig of Time brought its revenges. It is curious how history, public and private, repeats itself. The same harshness from which Roger Kemble had suffered he was afterwards to show to his own daughter, entertaining, like his own father-in-law, Ward, an objection to her marrying an actor, and especially a rather sorry and indifferent actor, with a poor worldly outlook. Be this as it may, a love affair caused Sarah Kemble to leave her home and take service in the house of Lady Greathead, at Guy's Cliff, near Warwick. Here she remained more than twelve months. Her father, relenting, gave his consent to her marriage with Henry Siddons, an actor in his company, 1773. Mrs. Siddons rose rapidly in her art. Garrick, hearing of her talent, engaged her at Drury Lane; she appeared in Portia. Her progress was not equal to her merits: this was attributed to the jealousy of the leading actresses. Garrick well knew her capabilities, but failed to encourage them; he gave her a trifling part, Venus, to look, not act, in a spectacle; very properly she refused to do it, and left the theatre, to return hereafter its pride and chief support, by her attraction. For thirty years no one disputed her supremacy. Nobility, gentry, public, all admired this gifted woman, and declared her worth—an ornament to the stage, an example in private life, loving and beloved. She retired from Drury Lane, June 29, 1812, at her farewell benefit playing Lady Macbeth, one of her great personations. On that memorable occasion the curtain fell on her sleeping scene. The audience would not see or hear anything more that night. She began with Shakespeare, and ended with him.

MRS. SIDDONS IN DUBLIN.—A bit of blarney from an old Irish newspaper : ' On Saturday, Mrs. Siddons, about whom all the world has been talking, exposed her beautiful face, her adamantine, soft, and lovely person, for the first time in Smock Alley Theatre, in the bewitching and all-tearful character of Isabella. ' From repeated panegyrics in the important London papers, we were taught to expect the sight of a heavenly angel ! But how were we supernaturally surprised into the most awful joy at the beholding a mortal goddess! She was nature itself. She was the most exquisite work of art. She was the very daisy, primrose, tuberose, sweet-briar, furze-blossom, gilly-flower, wall-flower, auricula, and rosemary; in short, she was the bouquet of Parnassus! not forgetting the holy three-leaved shamrock. Erin-go-bragh.—*Irish Post*, 1790'.

Mrs. Siddons died in Gower-street, June 8th, 1831, with a reputation never equalled, except by that of Garrick, on the English stage; mourned for by all who knew her worth and genius.

QUEEN CHARLOTTE AND MRS. SIDDONS.

ROYAL COMMAND.—Queen Charlotte, consort of George III., wished Mrs. Siddons to read to her, at Windsor Castle, some scenes from Shakespeare, and extracts from popular poets, occupying more than two hours. Mrs. Siddons was kept standing the whole time, so rigid was the German etiquette. Mrs. Siddons quitted the Royal presence, never to return. The next Royal command met with this decisive reply : 'That her readings and acting were public, and if her Majesty wished to hear her, Drury Lane Theatre must be the place, and no other.'

MRS. SIDDONS AND JOHN KEMBLE, at Bath, playing in ' Henry the Eighth.' Kemble, Cardinal Wolsey ; Mrs. Siddons, Queen Katharine. The power of Mrs. Siddons's eyes is well known, having so often been noticed by her biographers. On the occasion about to be related, their effect upon a young actor of the name of Davidge, acting the Surveyor to the Duke of Buckingham, was remarkable. At the words, 'The Duke shall govern England,' in a speech accusing his master, Buckingham, of treason to the King, Mrs. Siddons (Katharine), fixing her piercing gaze upon him ; he, kneeling with his back towards the audience, received the full force of her fiery flashing glances ·

' KATH. : Take good heed
    You charge not in your spleen a noble person,
    And spoil your noble soul. I say, take heed :
    Yea, heartily beseech you.'
' KING :   Let him on :
    Go forward.'

Not he, he was dumb ; such was the effect of Mrs. Siddons's eyes. Powerless with fright, the Surveyor remained transfixed to the ground. After a long pause, Kemble urged him to go on; the prompter repeatedly gave the words, ' On my soul, I'll speak the truth.' Neither truth nor falsehood could he utter with those terrible orbs, enraged, centred upon his timid face. The curtain was rung down amidst confusion and threats heaped upon the head of the unfortunate Davidge, who ran wildly out of the theatre, leaving Buckingham to be found guilty without his evidence.

DAVIDGE.

DAVIDGE, a native of Bath, lived to become an excellent actor, and manager of the Old Coburg and Surrey Theatres. He always retained in memory his first escapade, and resolved to redeem it. He carried this out by taking the Old Theatre Royal for two seasons, acting several of his best characters, Sir Peter Teazle, Justice Woodcock, etc., giving his townsfolk a taste of his quality.

AIKIN.

AIKIN, an actor of heavy business, nicknamed by his fellows Tyrant Aikin; noted for having fought a duel with John Kemble —pistols without balls—a topic for much ridicule in 1789.

JOHN PHILIP KEMBLE, 1757—1823.

JOHN PHILIP KEMBLE, educated at a Catholic seminary in Staffordshire, graduating at the Jesuits' College at Douay. His father, Roger Kemble, wished his son John to enter holy orders, and become a priest; but Fate had arranged matters otherwise. *Dis aliter visum.* He adopted the stage in place of stole and crozier— made his bow at Drury in 'Hamlet' in 1783. He was lessee of the theatre for a short period, playing Brutus, Coriolanus, Cato, etc., with a little pomposity (the fault of the age), and what we should now consider a tiresome elongation of words. Kemble sacrificed too much to art. During his management of Covent Garden the O.P. and P.S. riots commenced, arising from the alteration of prices of admission at Covent Garden. 'Black Jack' (such was his *sobriquet* among his theatrical brethren) taking this rebellion against his will to heart, retired to Switzerland, where he died in 1823.

Farewell Dinner to Mr. Kemble.—

LORD HOLLAND took his seat at the head table, with Mr. KEMBLE on his right, and the Duke of Bedford on his left hand. At the other tables, Mr. C. KEMBLE, Mr. YOUNG, and Mr. MATHEWS presided. The noble chairman gave 'THE KING,' 'THE PRINCE REGENT,' 'THE QUEEN and ALL the ROYAL FAMILY.' LORD HOLLAND then rose and said the Committee of management had agreed that he should have the honour of presenting the piece of plate which had been voted to Mr. Kemble; but, unfortunately, the exquisite workmanship of this production had caused it to be unprepared for public exhibition at the present moment. He had, however, a drawing and inscription, which he trusted the gentleman whom it was meant to honour would accept as an earnest of the vase itself. The inscription was: 'To John P. Kemble, on his retirement from the stage, of which, for thirty-six years, he had been the ornament and pride; which, to his learning, taste, and genius, was indebted for its present state of refinement (*great applause*), and which, under his auspices, consecrated to the support of the legitimate drama, and more particularly to the glory of Shakespeare (*applause*), attained to a degree of splendour and prosperity before unknown—this vase, from a numerous body of his admirers, as a mark of their gratitude and respect, was presented by the hands of their chairman on the 27th of June, 1817.' The noble Chairman, in a speech of considerable talent, remarked it had been observed by Mr. Sheridan, that the materials of an actor's fame were more perishable than those of any other artist; but the object of that meeting was to counteract this imperfection of the art (*applause*). Mr. Kemble had counteracted it, and as long as Shakespeare was remembered, Mr. Kemble could not be forgotten.

Mr. Young then recited some valedictory stanzas, written for the occasion by Mr. Campbell; after which the noble chairman proposed the health of Mr. Kemble, with three times three, which was drunk with enthusiasm.

'Pride of the British stage,
    A long and last adieu !
Whose image brought the heroic age
    Revived to Fancy's view.
Like fields refresh'd with dewy light,
    When the sun smiles his last,
Thy parting presence makes more bright
    Our memory of the past ;
And memory conjures feelings up,
    That wine or music need not swell,
As high we lift the festal cup,
    To Kemble—fare thee well !

'His was the spell o'er hearts,
    Which only Acting lends—
The youngest of the sister arts,
    Where all their beauty blends :
For ill can Poetry express
    Full many a tone of thought sublime;
And Painting, mute and motionless,
    Steals but a glance of Time.

> But by the mighty actor brought,
>   Illusion's perfect triumphs come,
> Verse ceases to be airy thought,
>   And Sculpture to be dumb.'

(Here the poem proceeds to portray the various personal and mental excellences of Mr. Kemble, excellences which fitted him to claim pre-eminence on the stage. His Cato, Hotspur, Othello, Henry V., and Lear are particularly noticed.)

> ' At once ennobled and correct,
>   His mind survey'd the tragic page,
> And what the actor could effect,
>   The scholar could presage.
>
> These were his traits of worth :
>   And must we lose them now ?
> And shall the scene no more show forth
>   His sternly-pleasing brow ?
> Alas, the moral brings a tear !—
>   'Tis all a transient hour below,
> And we that would detain thee here,
>   Ourselves as fleetly go !
> Yet shall our latest age
>   This parting scene review :
> Pride of the British stage,
>   A long and last adieu !'

After the recitation of the Ode, the four

last lines, set to music, were admirably sung :

> ' Yet shall our latest age
>> This parting scene review :
>> Pride of the British stage,
>> A long and last adieu ?'

Here Mr. Kemble rose and said, he begged them to accept his most grateful acknowledgments. It was a distinction which had never been bestowed on a predecessor, and he felt how much it was greater than his deserts. He accepted the tribute with pride and gratitude, and he flattered himself that he should be remembered when even that memorial had perished, since he had the good fortune to have his retirement from the stage celebrated by the Muse of the poets and the Genius of Music. He begged, in conclusion, to propose the health of their noble chairman, Lord Holland.

The health of Mr. Rae and Mr. Fawcett, and their respective companies, were drunk, and also of Mr. Campbell the poet, with applause.   They all returned thanks.

Lord HOLLAND said it was gratifying to see the union of feeling of the two rival theatres on this interesting occasion. There was present, however, a distinguished actor of a neighbouring country, and he should therefore propose ' the health of M. Talma, and success to the French stage,' with three times three, which was drunk with applause.

M. Talma spoke as follows : 'Gentlemen, it is impossible for a foreign language to express my warm gratitude for the hospitable way in which you have this day received me (*applause*), and the honour you have done, in my person, to the French stage.   To be thought worthy of notice on an occasion consecrated to my dear friend (*applause*), I estimate as one of the highest honours of my life.   As I cannot thank you with words, you will, I hope, suffer me to thank you with my heart (*applause*). Gentlemen, permit me to drink success to the British nation, and to the British stage (*applause*).

These few words, delivered in a clear and powerful voice, with great boldness of utterance and much action, had a great effect on the audience.

The health of Mr. West, and the Royal Academy, of Mr. Young, of Mrs. Siddons, and of Mr. Flaxman, were severally drunk.

Mr. Twiss returned thanks for Mrs. Siddons ; all the others being present spoke for themselves.

Lord HOLLAND then proposed the health of Mr. Mathews (who originally suggested the compliment to Mr. Kemble), and the committee who had so ably arranged the dinner. Mr. Mathews returned thanks in a speech at once neatly elegant and impressive, which was received with universal applause.

GEORGE FREDERICK COOKE, 1756—1812.

GEORGE FREDERICK COOKE.—First appeared in London in October 1800. A man of consummate dramatic genius, Nature had gifted this eccentric man with all the requisites for a great actor. Cooke by his misconduct and intemperate habits did much to destroy these natural endowments. No man ever held such a complete mastery over the passions as Cooke on the stage ; no man ever made less use of this power to secure lasting fame and fortune. Edmund Kean's style, without doubt, had been suggested by the performances of Cooke. Kean had seen his Richard, Sir Giles Overreach, etc., when a boy, and greatly resembled him in his acting.

Cooke, tempted by a good offer, and under the stress of calamitous circumstances, quitted England for America. On his way he played a few farewell nights at

Liverpool, his place of embarkation. The last performance was his favourite character of Richard the Third. Unfortunately he had indulged too freely in liquor, and played indifferently. This fact, which was quickly discovered by a full house, produced tokens of disapprobation, cries of 'shame,' hisses, etc. The irritated tragedian stalked down with offended dignity to the foot-lights, and thus addressed the audience :—

'Silence your clamour!' (*in a voice of thunder.*) 'I am George Frederick Cooke, the only tragic actor that you ever saw in your slave-trading town ; every brick of the accursed place is cemented by the blood of a negro!' and with these words he strode from the stage, never again to re-enter it. At that period the leading merchants of Liverpool were well-known slave-dealers, realising enormous fortunes by the unholy traffic.

Cooke died in America. Edmund Kean,

on his visit there, piously raised a tomb
to his memory.

RICHARD SUETT, 1758—1805.

DICKEY SUETT ('*Oh la! oh la!
Dickey!*'), a born droll; an immense
favourite with the pit and galleries of
Drury Lane. His exclamation, 'Oh la!'
heard behind the scenes, was quite sufficient
to set the house in a roar. Suett, originally
a baker, tired of his calling, tried the stage,
—a good exchange for Dickey. His Shakespearian clowns were held in high estimation with the critical frequenters of Old
Drury. His native humour, his queer
squeaking voice, his shuffling walk, and a
figure lank and tall, all went to make up
the droll effect. Suett managed to sustain
his popularity until death called him; even
then his love of fun did not desert him.
Lying on his bed, dying, he turned to a
friend sitting by him, and grasping his
hand, faintly chuckled :

'Oh la! Tom, don't you hear the rattles? the watchman's coming, I'm going; oh la l' (*trying to laugh*).

Suett alluded to the death-rattle in his throat. In those days watchmen carried rattles to alarm thieves.

On one occasion Dickey travelling from Bath to London, the coach was stopped on Hounslow Heath by a highwayman (an ordinary circumstance in those 'good old times'). The knight of the road demanded 'money or the passengers' lives.' Dreadfully alarmed, money, watches and jewellery were quickly given up. Suett screwed himself in a corner (*inside*).

Highwayman: 'Now, youngster, your purse. Money, or—' (*pistol presented*).

'Oh la! oh dear, sir, got none. "Nunkey"'' (*pointing to an elderly citizen*) 'pays for me' (*laughing idiotically*); 'oh la l'

With an oath the robber passed over

Dickey. 'Nunkey' sulked all the way to London, and on leaving the coach at the 'White Horse,' gave Suett a parting blessing—'Oh la!'

JOSEPH MUNDEN, 1758—1832.

MUNDEN.—After a rehearsal at Drury Lane, trudging home to Camden Town on a very wet day, carrying a seedy old gingham umbrella in one hand, three mackerel on a string in the other (Joey always studied economy, and found Clare Market cheaper than Camden Town), a gentleman stopped him to tell him how much he regretted that our comedian intended quitting the stage.

'Yes, yes, sir; I am going to bid you good-bye. Age, age, sir.'

' May I ask you to give me the smallest memento to remind me of the many happy hours your talents have yielded ? Just a trifle—I should so treasure it.'

' Eh, yes, I will ; take my umbrella, I'll take yours. Ha, ha !' (*chuckling*), 'now we shall never forget each other ; ha, ha ! Good-day, good-day ' (*looking at the silk*). ' Exchange is no robbery. Ha, ha ! I've done him !'

MUNDEN, staying to dine with CLINT the painter, suddenly called Clint's son : ' Harry, my dear boy, run home and tell Mrs. Munden not to take in the *Times* newspaper. I shall not be home ; that will save three half-pence, my boy. Run fast ! a penny saved is a penny earned ; ha, ha ! Make haste, dear.'

JACK BANNISTER, 1760—1836.

JACK BANNISTER, favourite pupil of Garrick, an excellent actor of Old Drury. Walter, in the ' Children of the Wood,' by the force of his acting became a part which all players coveted, and got to be considered as a test or touchstone of pathos

and comic humour. His Dick, in the
'Apprentice,' was full of life and vivacity.
Sheva, in the 'Jew,' a picture of man's
sordid nature ; miserly thrift could go no
further than when Sheva stoops to pick up
a pin, though in a furious passion. Colonel
Feignwell, in 'A Bold Stroke for a Husband,'
was one of his most effective parts. His
final appearance was as Echo, in the
comedy of 'The World,' at Drury Lane.

BILL OF DRURY LANE, 1791.—' Benefit
of Mr. Bannister, will be presented a
tragedy, called ·

' " RICHARD THE THIRD."

KING RICHARD, by *Mr. Bannister, junr.*
    (being his first appearance in that
    character, and for that night only).

KING HENRY, *Mr. Bensley.*
PRINCE OF WALES, *Miss de Camp.*
DUKE OF YORK, *Miss Standen.*

RICHMOND, *Mr. Palmer.*
BUCKINGHAM, *Mr. Williamson.*
NORFOLK, *Mr. Usher.*
RATCLIFFE, *Mr. Evatt.*
CATESBY, *Mr. Davis.*
TRESSELL, *Mr. Bland.*
OXFORD, *Mr. Chapman.*
STANLEY, *Mr. Aikin.*
BLUNT, *Mr. Lyons.*
TYRREL, *Mr. Rock.*
LORD MAYOR, *Mr. Blurton.*
FORREST, *Mr. Ledger.*
QUEEN, *Mrs. Whitfield.*
LADY ANNE, *Mrs. Kemble.*
DUCHESS OF YORK, *Mrs. Powell.*

' At the end of the tragedy a song called
" The Wolf," by Mr. Bannister ; to which
will be added

'" THE MAYOR OF GARRATT."

SIR JACOB JOLLAP, *Mr. Usher.*
MAJOR STURGEON, *Mr. Bannister* (with

the song of "O what a charming
thing's a battle!").
JERRY SNEAK, *Mr. Bannister, junr.* (with
the song of " What shall we have for
dinner," Mrs. Bond ?).
CRISPIN HEELTAP, *Mr. Burton.*
SNUFFLE, *Mr. Lyons.*
MRS. SNEAK, *Mrs. Webb.*
MRS. BRUIN, *Mrs. Powell.*'

1802.—Announcement in a Drury Lane
play-bill : ' MR. BANNISTER.—In consequence of his *confinement*, Mr. Bartley, at
a short notice, will take his part, Tandem,
in " The Marriage Promise," this evening,
May 7th, 1802.'

1809.—Copy of John Bannister's Budget
Bill :

' THEATRE ROYAL, IPSWICH.

Positively for one night only. Wednesday, November 29th, will be presented a

miscellaneous divertissement, with considerable vocal and rhetorical variations, called

'" BANNISTER'S BUDGET ;"

or, an Actor's Ways and Means: con-
sisting of songs and recitations, which will
be sung and spoken by Mr. Bannister, of
the Theatre Royal, Drury Lane.

'Prospectus of the divertissement :—
Part First: Exordium ; Mr. Bannis-
ter's Interview with Garrick ; Garrick's
Manner attempted in a Shaving Dialogue ;
Mr. Double-lungs in the Clay-pit ; Mack-
lin's Advice to his Pupils ; the Ship's
Chaplain and Jack Halyard and the Boat-
swain, or two ways of telling a story ; Sam
Stein, the Melodram Maniac, or value of
vocal talent ; Mr. and Mrs. O'Blunder, or
Irish Suicide.

'Part Second : Supernatural Sexton ;
Original Anecdotes of a late well-known
Character ; Trial and Cross-examination ;

Counsellor Garble ; Snip-Snap ; Serjeant Splitbrain's Address to the Jury ; Simon Soaker and Deputy Dragon.

' Part Third : Club of Queer Fellows ; President Hosier ; Speech from the Chair ; Mr. Hesitate ; Mr. Sawney McSnip ; Musical Poulterer ; Duet between a Game Cock and Dorking Hen ; Mr. Molasses ; Mr. Mince ; Monotony exemplified ; Mr. Killjoy ; the Whistling Orator ; Susan and Stephen. Budget closed. In Part three the Tragedy of " Othello" or Fine Fleecy Hosiery ; the Marrowfat Family ; Jollity burlesqued ; and Beggars and Ballad Singers.

' The doors open at six o'clock, to begin at seven. Boxes, 4*s.* Lower Circle, 3*s.* Pit, 2*s.* Gallery, 1*s.*

' N.B. Care has been taken to have the Theatre well aired. The whole entertainment has been arranged and revised by Mr. Colman ; the Songs principally composed by Mr. Reeve.'

DORA JORDAN, 1762—1816.

MRS. JORDAN (Miss Bland) born at Waterford, in Ireland, 1762. Her first English engagement was at York, with Tate Wilkinson, as Mrs. Jordan. In Dublin she had acted under the name of 'Miss Francis.' She appeared at Drury Lane in 1785, in 'The Country Girl,' at a salary of £4 per week. The highest payment that she received in the zenith of her popularity was £25 weekly. What would leading Metropolitan ladies say to that in these days of extravagant salaries and conditions so detrimental to managers' interests ? Dorothy Jordan played all and everything—tragedy, comedy, opera and farce. But there is no question that comedy was her forte; all her great successes were Thalia's —Viola, Lady Contest, Lady Teagle, Miss Hardcastle, Little Pickle, Lydia Languish, Rosalind, etc. It is supposed that no

woman ever spoke humorous speeches
like her. She was quite as attractive as
Peg Woffington, and had a much sweeter
voice, but was not so handsome. But she
excelled all others. Her connexion with
the Duke of Clarence, afterwards William
IV., continued for twelve years, but
ended for poor Dorothy's feeling, loving
heart unhappily. A separation became
imperative, the Royal Duke being on the
eve of marriage with the late Queen
Adelaide. The once-cherished actress
stood in the way. General Charitie, a
personal friend and confidant of the Duke's,
was entrusted with the delicate, unpleasant
task of breaking the news so fatal to her
happiness. Mrs. Jordan was acting in
Cheltenham when Charitie saw her. A
most painful scene ensued. The injured
woman, almost frantic, would listen to no
proposals, excuses, or offers of settlement
 No, no! not a penny. Why did he not

come himself and do his dirty work ? No.' She was compelled to give up her engagements—quitted Cheltenham for London, in a state of bewilderment ; her wounded pride struggling with her love for her children, in after years ennobled by their royal father; she sought repose in a foreign land. In France, unknown and neglected, she lived for awhile upon her little savings—a mere pittance (for Dorothy Jordan's purse had always been opened to every appeal in the days of her prosperity) ; and there she died without one friend to solace or comfort her, and was buried at the expense of an English gentleman who had formerly been an admirer of her acting.

BENJAMIN CHARLES INCLEDON, 1764—1826.

INCLEDON (1826), celebrated bass-singer. His rendering of Dibdin's sea-songs won golden opinions from all in that age of patriotism. Incledon was rather too much given to indulgence in wine, and began to lose his fine voice. Elliston saw this, and remonstrated. Incledon always attributed it to sore-throats, colds, etc. He was frequently obliged to omit his best songs. This occurred so many times, that his manager grew restive.

'Incledon, you have lost your voice.'

SINGER: 'Have I, governor? Perhaps you'll tell me who's found it?'

MARY ROBINSON (DIED 1800).

MRS. ROBINSON (Miss Darby), born in Bristol—much cared for by Hannah More in youth—for some time taught as a governess, being compelled to earn her living from her father's having deserted his home. At the early age of sixteen she married a Mr. Robinson, a lawyer. Careless and extravagant, his fortune was soon spent, and want forced her to apply to Garrick for employment on the stage. She

came out at Drury Lane in 1776, as Juliet.
Her beauty and ability at once established
her with the public as a favourite ; no one
had made such an impression on the stage
since Peg Woffington's retirement.   A
royal command was given for the 'Winter's
Tale,' in which she played Perdita—dressing, looking, and acting so well as to
charm all hearts, including that of George,
Prince of Wales.   His Royal Highness fell
madly in love with this lovely woman, sign-
ing himself 'Florizel,' when he wrote to
his 'Perdita.'   The Prince gave her his
likeness and all the heart he possessed.
Poor Perdita's husband, living in idle de-
bauchery on her earnings, totally neglected
her.   Tempted by exalted rank, ardent
love, and a fortune to be settled upon her,
she quitted the stage to live under the
protection of a worthless deceiver.   The
Prince deserted her, never paid the annuity
promised, and even shunned her in the

streets.   She wrote novels, poems for news-
papers, magazines, etc., and died in 1800,
in adverse circumstances.

CHARLES DIGNUM, 1765—1827.

CHARLES DIGNUM, vocalist, transplanted
from Vauxhall Gardens to Drury Lane. A
buck *à la mode* was Dignum.   His ballads
were much relished by pit and gallery
frequenters.

SAMUEL RUSSELL, 1766—1845.

'JERRY SNEAK' RUSSELL.—One part
made Russell, viz., Jerry Sneak in 'The
Mayor of Garratt.'   He tried high comedy
first, but found his ambition soared too
lofty, so reduced his views to low comedy,
and became a universal favourite with the
public.

EDWARD KNIGHT, 1774—1826.

LITTLE KNIGHT.—Capital 'country boy'
in old comedies ; his comic singing pleased
greatly.   Songs for Knight were intro-

duced in all pieces, and encores were certain. He came to Drury from Tate Wilkinson's York circuit.

JOHN COOPER (BORN 1770).

JOHN COOPER, 'respectable John,' careful and prudent, always looking well to the main chance ; a sort of small Talleyrand in theatricals, keeping his position with every managerial change, and they were many. Cooper was born at Bath, and made his first stage-effort in that beautiful city of thermal waters, rich dowagers, and decayed gentry. After the customary wanderings, privations, etc., that poor players are heirs to, 'respectable' John found himself in London, enlisted under the banners of Elliston for Old Drury, generally playing second parts in comedy and tragedy, and first in the absence of better men, such as Macready, Young, Elliston, etc. Painstaking and polite, stage-management awaited him. Increased salary, and un-disturbed authority naturally followed. He retired after fifty years' service, well-to-do in a worldly sense, and much respected. When Macready returned from America, and appeared at the Princess's, Cooper was engaged to act the second characters to him. ' Hamlet ' was the opening play. *Hamlet*, Mr. Macready ; *Ghost*, Mr. Cooper. Macready was very particular about his ghostly father's dress, always furnishing it himself. In the scene where Hamlet follows his sire to the ramparts of Elsinore Castle, at the moment when the spirit proclaims himself Hamlet's buried father, Cooper started and rubbed his neck, proceeding, ' Thy father's spirit, doomed for a certain time to—— ' Another jerk of his ghostly head. (*Aside*), ' What the devil is it ?'

MACREADY *(groaning with rage):* 'Go on, sir.'

'I cannot; I'm ate up alive by something,' wriggling and twisting his body—audience laughing.

TRAGEDIAN : 'Get off, sir.'

COOPER : 'Where's the trap?' (to lead to sulphurous flames)—feeling with his foot for it—descends, rubbing his back. 'Oh, remember me !'

Macready, in a towering passion, rushed to the green-room when the act-drop fell, demanding an explanation of John for his strange conduct.

'Ask the cockroaches in your infernal armour.'

It was discovered on search to be swarming with cockroaches, never having been unpacked until that night since it was used in America.

A MOULTING GHOST. — 'Respectable John' indulged his health and purse by starring during the vacations. One night, while acting 'Hamlet' at Portsmouth for a

Jewish Society's Benefit, the following ludi-
crous incident occurred : The leading actor
of the company, rather prone to over-dress
in his characters, personated the Ghost.
Resolved to look 'the buried Majesty of
Denmark' like a king, he borrowed from
a friendly undertaker a number of black
feathers used in his business. These huge
trappings of woe were attached to the
ghostly helmet. When Hamlet encoun-
tered his father's spirit, a feather dropped
on the stage ; slowly crossing the stage,
down came another. The audience tit-
tered. Beckoning his royal son to follow
him, all the sable plumes fell on the stage.
This was too much for the Jews. A shrill
voice shouted, ' Ikey, Ikey, look at that !
Blow'd if the ghost ain't a-moulting his
feathers !' Very little more of ' Hamlet '
was heard that night.

JOHN BRAHAM, 1774—1856.

JOHN BRAHAM (of Jewish extraction).—
This first of English vocalists surmounted
difficulties that beset his youth, which
might have proved fatal to many less
energetic. He was of a very humble
origin, and his education had been neglected. He was obliged to earn his daily
bread at an early age. Nevertheless,
John Braham, gifted with a superb voice
and pure musical taste, and assisted by
benevolent friends, who saw the boy's
merit, was in a few years acknowledged to
be the first tenor singer in Great Britain,
thanks to his instructor, Leoni Lee, and to
his own untiring industry. The English
Opera never before had such a vocalist.
From his exertions it became popular, and
was patronised by all classes. George
IV. held Braham in high esteem, frequently honouring Drury Lane by a Royal

command when he sang. I was present at one of these. The King selected 'The Devil's Bridge.' Opulence, position, and fame attended our great vocalist's progress; blessed with a charming wife, and a family of clever children. In an unlucky hour he tempted fortune, hitherto so bountiful, by building a stately theatre in King-street, St. James's, at the large outlay of £36,000. This elegant establishment Braham opened under his own management, reaping nothing but disappointment and vexation for his pains. Charles Dickens wrote three successive dramatic pieces (burlettas and comic operas) for the St. James's Theatre. The first was 'The Strange Gentleman,' a comic burletta, founded on one of the 'Sketches by Boz,' performed for the first time on September 29, 1836; and this was followed by the comic opera of 'The Village Coquettes,' played for the first time in December of the same year.

A third attempt, the least known of the three, entitled ' Is She his Wife? or Something Singular,' was produced in March, 1837. These were all more or less successful at the time, and ran for a considerable number of nights. All three of them have appeared in print.[*]

During his management of the St. James's Theatre, Braham wanted to produce my piece, 'The Blue Jackets,' on liberal terms. He proffered to act and sing in it.

' St. James's Theatre.

'DEAR STIRLING,

  ' I will play the Admiral in your piece, and introduce "Wapping Old Stairs." I have not acted a new part for years.

' Yours,
' JOHN BRAHAM.

' Mr. Stirling,

 ' Adelphi Theatre.'

---

[*] See ' The Bibliography of Dickens. A Bibliographical List of the Published Writings in Prose and Verse of Charles Dickens,' by Richard Herne Shepherd (1880), pp. 8-9.

Braham's talents for singing became a heritage with his sons. They were all good singers, and held positions on the Metropolitan stage, Italian and English Opera.

Why St. James's Theatre was built.—Braham, our first tenor, during the height of his popularity at Drury Lane, among many other privileges, exacted a private box every night that he appeared in a new opera. This box, expressly for the use of Mrs. Braham (a lady inclined to *embonpoint*), was stipulated to be on the pit tier, to avoid the inconvenience of going upstairs. At the first representation of ' William Tell ' at the English Opera, Braham as Tell, there was an overflowing house; not a box nor place to be had. Mrs. Braham presented herself at the Box Office. Alas! her box had been let to a duchess. Mrs. Braham, highly offended, had to mount to the upper circle, a small box, two steps to reach it from the corridor. Making this descent, the lady slipped, dislocating her ankle, and was immediately conveyed home. Braham never forgave Bunn for this, promising his wife that she should have a theatre of her own, never to be disappointed again. He built the St. James's Theatre at a cost of nearly £40,000, and managed it himself at a loss of £20,000 in three years; total, £60,000 for a slip of the foot.

JOHN LISTON, 1776—1846.

LISTON came out at the Haymarket as Sheepface in 'The Village Lawyer,' in 1805. He had previously been a school-master at Gosport, and an usher at St. Martin's School, Charing Cross. Liston, like many other low comedians, fancying that he could act tragedy—tried Hamlet, Romeo, etc. Fortunately for himself and the public, he speedily discovered his mistake. Liston's face, quite stolid manner, and innate drollery, at once stamped the comedian. For many years he appeared at Drury Lane, Covent Garden, Haymarket, and a brief season at the Olympic, after his retirement, to introduce the son of his old friend Charles Mathews to the stage,—Charles Mathews, junior, acting with him at a salary of £100 per week, paid by Madame Vestris. Liston's Paul Pry took the town by surprise. 'I hope I don't intrude' became the joke of the day. The Prince Regent, afterwards George IV., was a great admirer of Liston's grotesque fun. On one occasion the King gave a command for 'The Hypocrite' at Drury Lane, and honoured Liston by going in state to laugh at his Mawworm. His Majesty, convulsed with laughter, encored the celebrated Sermon twice, joined by the whole house. Nothing could exceed the effect and comic humour that Liston threw into this preaching to old Lady Lambert's servants in the kitchen—pulpit, a clothes' horse covered with a tablecloth ; chair behind ; cook, housemaids, footman, etc., seated before it. Liston, imitating a well-known Wesleyan minister, harangued them with threats of their damnation, telling them that they would be d——d (*deep groans*). When he went up! up! up! they would go down! down! down! Then would they cry out and try to cling to his coat-tails to go up—no, he'd serve 'em all out by cutting 'em off, and wear a spencer (fashionable jacket of the time). King and people yelled again at this irresistibly comic situation, his Majesty throwing himself back in his chair and screaming with delight. Liston died in 1846, rich.

LISTON AT A CITY GENT'S DINNER-PARTY.—Dining-out, as a rule, Liston disliked ; but on a certain occasion he yielded to the earnest solicitations of a member of the Stock Exchange. A numerous party were assembled to meet the comedian, naturally expecting a fund of anecdote, jokes, and racy humour from the lips of this high-priest of Momus. Liston ate his dinner without exchanging a word; this cast a gloom over the visitors. After a pause, young Hopeful, the host's youngest boy, sitting by Liston, pinched his arm, whispering : ' Do say something funny to make us laugh, like you do on the stage. Ma didn't want players, but Pa insisted— said you were the " biggest fish in the market, not easily hooked " — do be funny !' Be sure, Paul Pry never intruded at Chesham-place again.

HARRIET MELLON (Duchess of St. Albans), 1775—1837.

HARRIET MELLON (Mrs. Coutts, and afterwards Duchess of St. Albans), born 1775.—This clever lady had an invete-rate dislike to Poland and the Poles, engendered by her nephew Lord Dudley

Stuart's persistent appeal to the public for funds to enable the Poles to carry out their attempt to overthrow the Russian yoke. Yates produced a drama at the Adelphi called 'Burning of Moscow and Liberation of Poland.' The Duchess of St. Alban's in her box on the first night, speedily quitted it, in a towering passion.

'Yates. Yates! why did you bring me here? I have enough of the Poles at home. Curse the Poles! they'll haunt me to my grave.'

She drove off with anything but blessings on the 'Fair Land of Poland,' and much to the chagrin of the manager, who basked in her smiles and purse. The Duchess was a good friend to Frederick Yates on and off the stage.

CHARLES YOUNG, 1777—1856.

CHARLES YOUNG, a disciple of the Kemble school, first acted in public in

1807. Majestic in gait, slow and serious in declamation, he was very like John Kemble. All Young's speeches were delivered with effect; well studied and graceful, but lacked the touch of nature so essential to carry an audience away. In Brutus, Joseph Surface, Iago, Lord Townley, Falkland, etc., Young was excellent; his very defects told in these characters. He died in 1856, after a long and enjoyable retirement from his mimic world.

JOHN EMERY, 1777—1822.

JOHN EMERY, an admirable representative of countrymen, more especially Yorkshiremen. Emery possessed the reputation of being the best actor in his line that ever appeared. He was for one season only at Drury Lane. Covent Garden carried away this genuine actor, and wisely retained his services. Parts were written expressly for him, and playwrights courted the representative of Zekiel Homespun, Tyke in ' The School of Reform,' Giles, in ' The Miller's Man,' Fixture, Robin Rough head, Farmer Ashfield. He was equally good in Shakespearian characters, such as Caliban, Sir Toby Belch, etc. Emery was an artist of no mean ability; his water-colour drawings realised attention, and fair prices. He came from York, Tate Wilkinson's excellent school for actors. He quitted the stage and this life, 1822, universally regretted by lovers of true acting.

SAMUEL EMERY, son of John Emery, inherits a large portion of his father's talent in the same line—countrymen and character parts. Everything Sam Emery touches dramatically impresses his audiences with truth to nature. Even in the smallest detail of character this excellent quality is worked out. Hence Emery is liked and followed, always a good name in a bill.

Wide is the range of Emery's *rôle*, embracing old and young men, countrymen, sailors, ' heavy fathers,' eccentric comedy, etc. In the plays adapted from the novels of Charles Dickens he found genial employment ; his personations of Prowdie, Fagin, Peggotty, Captain Cuttle, Peerybingle, Jonas Chuzzlewit, will not be forgotten. Nearly all the London theatres have availed themselves of Emery's abilities. He tried America a few years since, and a second tour enabled Australia to enjoy a really good actor. The result proved equally satisfactory to the entertainers and the entertained.

JOSEPH GRIMALDI.

JOEY GRIMALDI, first of all clowns—last of the genuine pantomimic humourists. Grimaldi did more to create fun with a string of paper sausages than modern clowns do with the most expensive properties. The chief and standing joke now-adays is for Motley to knock and kick about policemen. Music-hall breakdowns, songs of questionable character, and constant utterance of the silliest nonsense, making up for real acting and rapid invention—attributes of clowns of the old school. John Kemble was wont to observe that Grimaldi was the best low comedian he had ever seen—high praise, coming from such a source. Most clever was Joey's impromptu carriage-building : a clothes-basket, two broom-handles, a cheese-rolling-pin ; lastly, an umbrella—all the articles purloined, of course, slyly, not openly ; and here you had a carriage extempore that would have puzzled Long-Acre coach-makers to build. Joey's fertile brain con-verted seeming impossibilities into pos-sibilities with the rapidity of lightning. At Grimaldi's last painting of the face and attempt to sing his once-famous song,

'Hot Codlins,' poor Joey, broken down by age and illness, was carried on the stage of Sadler's Wells in an arm-chair to say 'Farewell.' The sight was a painful one, to witness the total decadence of him who had contributed so largely in mirth to the merry Christmases of years gone by. The old man's spirits, memory and humour were things of the past.

JOEY GRIMALDI and VESTRIS, the celebrated French dancer. Joey envied the foreign artiste's talent, especially the long time that he danced on one leg.

'Ah, that's nothing,' said Motley, 'to my old performing goose ; he'll stand on one of his legs five minutes, flap his wings and cackle ; that's what Monsieur Frenchman can't do.'

GRIMALDI.—Pantomime, 'Fortunatus,' Drury Lane. A utility actor was selected to join a procession of petrified figures. At a certain cue, standing at a wing, he was ordered by the prompter to go on.

REPLY : ''Tis not my turn, sir. I am not to go on till Mr. Grimaldi's *putrefied.'*

RICHARD JONES, 1778—1851.

RICHARD JONES.—A worthy successor of Lewis in high and eccentric legitimate comedy, one of the most painstaking dressers the stage ever had. Fashion and first-rate tailors did much for our comedian's exquisite figure. Jones seldom remained still a moment when engaged in a scene, always bustling about, to the great distress of some of his fellow-actors. Mercutio, Roderigo, the Copper Captain, Jeremy Diddler and Rover, proved that Jones had well filled his friend Lewis's position in public opinion. Added to his acting, Jones instructed pupils for the Bar, Church, and State.

TOM COOKE, 1781—1848.

T. P. COOKE, last and best of stage sailors, too frequently rendered ridiculous

by the introduction of silly terms and *outré*
habits, unknown to real tars. Cooke
possessed one great advantage. He had
in reality trod the deck of a man-of-war,
and passed through the perils of shipwreck,
battle, and storm. He loved the sea :

> 'The sea ! the sea !
> The blue, the fresh, the ever free !'

Having served as a cabin boy with
Nelson's fleet at Copenhagen, it is little
wonder that his personification of a British
sailor excelled and surpassed all others.
Long Tom Coffin (Pilot); William, in
' Black-Eyed Susan,' played in every town
in the United Kingdom with applause and
profit.—Drury Lane and Covent Garden
readily opened their doors to receive
William and his Susan—dancing (horn-
pipes), fighting, singing. Cooke always at
home, a pantomimist of the first rank.
Monster in ' Frankenstein,' Vampire,
Zamiel in ' Der Freischütz,' and Vander-

decken in the 'Flying Dutchman,' were one, and all studies of art and dramatic skill. After many years' labour, he amassed a large fortune. Strict economy governed Cooke's actions from the beginning until the end. When he commenced travelling with a Circus, at a modest salary of fifteen shillings a week, he saved. Well do I remember his kind and useful admonition to myself: 'Stirling, my boy, be frugal; keep a nest-egg; proportion your expenses to what you earn, not to your expectations.' Sage counsel!

Story of Tom Cooke's appearance in 'DER FREISCHÜTZ;' composer, Karl Von Weber.— This marvellous and weird musical creation, a work of true genius, created a profound sensation in the musical world, and became the subject of gossip in every city of Europe and America. Operas, theatres, assembly-rooms, artists, drawing-rooms, pianos, organs, street-singers, street-boys' whistles, re-echoing the famous Hunting Chorus, 'Hark, follow I hark, follow I' Bridesmaids' Chorus ; ballad, 'Sweet Agnes :' everybody that could sing did sing. Words would fail adequately to describe the effect produced on the public by the incantation music in the 'Haunted Glen.' This opera, in a dramatic form, with some of the music, was first acted in England at the English Opera House, Strand (now the Lyceum).   Original cast :

CASPER, *Mr. G. Bennett.*
ROLLO, *Mr. H. Phillips.*
ADOLPH, *Pearman.*
KILLIAN, *Keeley and Taylure.*
ZAMIEL, *Mr. T. P. Cooke* ⎫ Playing the Hunt-
HEAD RANGER, *Mr. Baker* ⎬ ing Chorus on a
ANNE, *Miss Noel.* ⎭ shepherd's pipe.
AGNES, *Miss Povey.*

First cast at Drury Lane :
ADOLPH, *Tom Cooke.*

CASPER, *Charles Horn.*
ROLLO, *Paul Bedford,*
OTTOCAR, *Mercer.*
KILLIAN, *Keeley.*
ZAMIEL., *O. Smith.*
AGNES, *Miss Stephens.*
ANNE, *Miss Cawse.*

FIRST NIGHT : Set scene for ' Enchanted Glen.' Lofty rocks on each side surrounding the glen ; stunted trees ; torrents ; a fragile bridge thrown across the stage from rocks on the left to rocks on the right ; this bridge at least twenty-four feet high from the stage, to reach which, after crossing the bridge over a torrent, a rude flight of steps, composed of stones, ivy, trees, etc. Adolph sings on the bridge. Casper, below in the glen, preparing a charmed circle for infernal bullet-casting. Music unearthly ; moon obscured by red ; owls and bats joining in diabolical chorus.

Cooke (*Adolph*), very nervous, reached the bridge, stopped, sang his ballad, ' Gentle Agnes,' on the rocks, not daring to venture on the bridge.   There stood Cooke trembling.

Horn (*Casper*) (*speaking through his music*): 'Come down, Tom, you'll be too late' (*music*).

Cooke : ' Bedad, Charley, I can't.   Not a fut of me will move.'

Horn (*terrified at the consequence to the opera*) : ' You must, you'll ruin the scene. The bridge is safe enough.'

Cooke (*loud*): ' Is it? By holy Moses, you'd better come up and try, Charley ; it's got the staggers.'

Casper and Zamiel cast the seven bullets with attendant horrors of ghosts, demons, fiery skulls, swords, skeleton hunt through the air, torrents of blood, curtain of fire, Devil himself, but no Tom Cooke in the magic circle.   He remained on the rock, holding hard by a tree, while he sang, trembling.

JULIA GLOVER, 1781—1850.

MRS. GLOVER, born in Ireland, in 1781, commenced her theatrical life before she was out of her teens. Pretty Julia won the hearts of her loving countrymen. Nothing came amiss to our young actress—Juliet, Cordelia, The Romp, Little Pickle; at times, for her benefits and her father's pockets, Romeo and Hamlet. This gifted woman, the very soul of humour, rapidly reached that goal, coveted by all Thespian followers, Drury Lane. Here she found a fitting field for her remarkable talents. An unlucky marriage with a careless spendthrift, Captain Glover; a young family entirely dependent on her savings for their support; debts continually paid for her husband's extravagance, made sad havoc with her home comforts. Still Julia Glover worked loyally on, playing a varied

round of characters in every description of
piece—tragedy, comedy, farce, burlesque,
all well done, many excellent ; few could
compare with Mrs. Glover. Mrs. Candour,
Mrs. Heidelberg, Widows Warren and
Green, Mrs. Malaprop, Mrs. Hardcastle,
the Nurse in ' Romeo and Juliet,' Lucretia
MacTab, and many other characters, in
her hands became irresistibly comic—such
bright sparkling humour, never flagging,
was hers! She enjoyed acting ; her heart
was in it. A loving mother, perhaps a
trifle careless of her pecuniary affairs ; in
her old age she wanted help. Her purse
had never been closed to those that asked.
Mrs. Glover's salary never reached £20
a week in the zenith of her popularity.
Trouble and sickness disabled the poor
care-worn actress. An appeal to the public
was generously responded to in the shape
of a substantial benefit, £1,000. It came
too late ; she died on the very night the

benefit took place. While her professional brothers and sisters were acting on her behalf, she passed quietly away, leaving a gap in the theatrical ranks not easily filled up.

MRS. BARTLEY, 1785—1850.

MRS. BARTLEY (Miss Smith), born 1785. —The only lady that effectually opposed or rivalled Mrs. Siddons in her supremacy of tragedy. I was acting at Richmond with Klanert, her brother-in-law, when Mrs. Bartley came to play *Mrs. Beverly* in 'The Gamester.' I had a small part allotted me—Dawson, rather particular in one scene with Mrs. Beverly. At the termination of the play, I was asked to go into the green-room. Here I found all the company assembled with my manager and Mrs. Bartley : 'Young gentleman,' said the lady, addressing me, 'I have sent for you to thank you, and express my opinion publicly of your refined and excellent performance this evening of a highly essential though trivial part. I never heard anything more beautifully delivered than your reading. Go on, sir; believe me, you will become a great actor.' Alas! her kind words were never destined to be realised. Mrs. Bartley retired from the stage several years before she died: the evening of her days was blessed with a loving husband and a happy home.

WILLIAM FARREN, 1786—1861.

WILLIAM FARREN (born 1786), a polished actor, and true type of fashionable society. —Farren's Lord Ogleby in ' The Clandestine Marriage ' would have done honour to Beau Nash, or Brummel. Farren dressed and acted his characters to perfection—a gentleman of the old school—so neat, so precise, one always felt that he had walked out of a gallery of family pictures. His Sir Peter Teazle bore the palm from all his brother artists. Phelps was the nearest approach to Farren's Sir Peter. After a prosperous career at the Haymarket, Covent Garden, and Drury Lane, he tried his hand at management at the Strand and the Olympic. In this, good fortune did not attend his efforts. It should be noted that it was he who introduced to the public at the Olympic a remarkable man, ' Little Robson.'

WILLIAM FARREN, junior, son to this excellent actor, succeeds to his father's ability and station worthily on and off the stage. Witness his performances in ' Our Boys,' Old Dornton, Sir Peter Teazle at the Vaudeville, where his acting adds not a little to the excellence of all the pieces that he is called upon to take part in.

JOHN PRITT HARLEY, 1786—1858.

JOHN PRITT HARLEY (born 1786) wore the cap and bells of Momus at Drury for thirty years. He appeared in 1815 as Lissardo, in 'The Wonder;' and quitted the profession he had so long and well adorned at the Princess's under Charles Kean's management. Eccentric and thrifty to all outward appearance, Harley died penniless. He had a passion for collecting walking-sticks, canes, etc., and when he died, more than three hundred were sold, from golden heads to humble ash and thorn.

FANNY KELLY (BORN 1790).

FANNY KELLY appeared at the Haymarket, 1808. Engaged at Arnold's English Opera House, she left it to act at Drury Lane. Her style was one full of deep feeling, strictly copied from her model, Nature; with a genuine humour in comedy, ranging over a vast diversity of characters, from Lady Teazle to Madge in ' Love in a Village.' Everything she acted was equally good. In what is now termed the ' sensational ' drama, no one ever surpassed Fanny Kelly. Her Mary in ' The Innkeeper's Daughter,' her Gil Blas, above all her acting in a drama called ' The Sergeant's Wife,' was so terribly real that her audience appeared spell-bound—a scene in which she was supposed to see a murder committed through crevices in the walls of a wretched hovel was most appalling. After saving a considerable fortune, she unhappily lost part of it by the fraudulent acts of a trusted banker, and by a venture in which she unluckily embarked, of converting a building into a theatre—the Royalty, Dean-street, Soho, in which she acted. This proved a bad investment for Fanny Kelly and her fortunes. The following is a copy of the programme of her farewell benefit :

' THEATRE ROYAL, DRURY LANE.

MISS KELLY.

FAREWELL BENEFIT.

'This evening, Monday, June 8, 1835, Wycherley's Comedy of the

'"COUNTRY GIRL."

MOODY, *Mr. F. Mathews.*

BELVILLE, *Mr. Wood.*

HARCOURT, *Mr. Cooper.*

SPARKISH (for this night only), *Mr. Harley.*

WILLIAM, *Mr. Mears.*

COUNTRYMAN, *Mr. F. Mathews.*

MISS PEGGY (the Country Girl), *Miss Kelly.*

ALETHEA, *Mrs. Vining.*

LUCY, *Mrs. F. Mathews.*

'MR. HARLEY will sing his popular mock bravura :

"Oh Dolce Doll concento," and "Johnny Bond."

'The popular drama called the

'"SERGEANT'S WIFE."

OLD CARTOUCHE, *Mr. F. Mathews.*

GASPARD, *Mr. O. Smith.*

YOUNG CARTOUCHE, *Mr. Wood.*

Sergeant Louis, *Mr. Mears.*

Robin, *Mr. Keeley.*

Dennis (for this night only), *Mr. Evans.*

Lisette (the Sergeant's wife), *Miss Kelly.*

Margot, *Mrs. Keeley.*

'At the end of the second piece, Miss Kelly will deliver a farewell address.

'The musical arrangements under the direction of Mr. T. Cooke:

Mr. Templeton—Ballad, by desire, "Black-Eyed Susan."

Mr. H. Phillips — Ballad, "Woman" (Wither, 1650).

Mr. Wilson—Ballad, "John Anderson my Jo."

Miss Fanny Healy—Song, "Lo, Gentle Lark," accompanied on the flute by Mr. Price.

Mrs. H. R. Bishop—Song, "Auld Robin Gray."

Miss Bruce—Song, "I can nowhere find my Laddie."

Miss Clara Novello—Song, "Let the bright Seraphim," accompanied on the trumpet by Mr. Handly.

Mr. Bennett—Aria, "Tu vedrai" from "La Sventurata."

'To conclude with the favourite farce,

'"Turning the Tables."

Jeremiah Bumps, *Mr. Cooper.*
Jack Humphreys, *Mr. Harley.*
Edgar de Courcy, *Mr. Wood.*
Thornton, *Mr. Henry.*
Mr. Knibbs, *Mr. Hughes.*
Mrs. Humphreys, *Mrs. Broad.*
Miss Knibbs, *Mrs. East.*
Patty Larkins, *Mrs. Fitzwilliam.*'

RAYNER.

Rayner, a Yorkshire Tyke, fond of running horses, a good actor in character parts, countrymen and Scotchmen ; Tyke, in the 'School of Reform;' Giles, in 'The Miller's Maid ;' Dougal. But through racing and the 'Corner' (Tattersall's), constant visits to Newmarket, Doncaster, Epsom, etc., backing fields and favourites, poor Rayner was brought to a low ebb. His betting had proved abortive, his race run, terminating with a *dead* heat, in poverty and disappointment.

BRISCOE.

A BLIND MANAGER.—Briscoe, an actor of small charades at Drury Lane, quitted the theatre for strolling management ; unfortunately became blind, yet acted all the heroes in tragedy, and lovers in comedy, for many years. — *Wolverhampton Chronicle*, 1792.

CHARLES MATHEWS, THE ELDER
1775—1835.

CHARLES MATHEWS, the elder, was born in the Strand. His father was a Wesleyan bookseller, much averse to plays and players ; not so his hopeful son. When a boy he used to act tragedies in a loft with reprobate school-fellows, unknown to their parents. Time crept on, and despite the old bookseller's exordiums, Mathews ran away from his home, and joined a troop of wandering actors. Tate Wilkinson admitted him into his company, in their circuit of York, Hull, Lincoln, etc. Here Mathews found a kind instructor, and a thorough training school for the London boards. When his time arrived, he appeared at Drury Lane ; at once the town recognised a clever man. This reputation he never lost ; it increased yearly. His solo entertainments stood unrivalled for genuine humour, singing, and joyous gaiety ; mail-coach adventures, trips to Paris, etc.; Monsieur Mallet, an old French *emigré;* Mathews made a feature of his tenderness and eccentricity to such perfection that it filled the Adelphi Theatre nightly for many months.

Goldfinch, Ollapod, Mawworm, Lingo, Jubal in 'The Jew,' Crabtree, Dr. Pangloss, and scores of equally important characters he played with finish and artistic skill,—a student always in the art he so much graced.

CHARLES MATHEWS, THE YOUNGER, 1803—1878.

CHARLES MATHEWS, the clever son of a clever sire. Query, did Momus officiate at Charley's christening—bestowing those priceless gifts, fun, frolic, and untiring vivacity? Mathews possessed all, and retained them to the end; one of the most popular of modern actors, his appearance on the stage a provocative to laughter. Time seemed to have forgotten him, so lightly had his hand touched Mathews. Astonishing vitality and unceasing flow of spirits; appearance youthful, walk, manner as of yore; constantly on the move, reaping golden harvests. Worldly cares never disturbed, nor disappointments vexed his mind. Always a smile and merry jest, immense range of versatility, inimitable humour and quick perception, seizing every point available to produce fun,—witness his Affable Hawk, Marplot, Sir Charles Coldstream, and a host of other side-splitting creations. He undertook a voyage to India in his seventieth year, America, Australia, Paris; always on the move. His first appearance on the public stage was at the Olympic, of which Madame Vestris, his future wife, was manageress, in a piece written by Leman Rede, called ' The Old and Young Stager.' Old Stager, Liston ; Young Stager, Charles Mathews. A complete success attended this effort. Lyceum, Covent Garden Theatres, conjointly with Vestris, he managed for a series of years. His second wife was an American lady, a capital actress in comedy. Resolved to work until the last. Mathews

still continued to delight his hosts of admirers. Haymarket, Drury Lane, Gaiety;
his final engagement was at Manchester.
In harness this remarkable man died, June
24th, 1878, aged seventy-five; pretty well
for a light comedian!

CHARLES MATHEWS and his poetic milkman.—Charley never at home to payments
in general, especially tradesmen's! A long
score for milk—no returns. Charles always
too busy to attend to milk. The dairy-
man, driven to his wits' end, sent the
following affecting appeal by post:

> 'Mr. Mathews, sir, pay my bill,
> My pockets are empty, so's my till.
> You've my milk, pure and sweet,
> Without money my cows can't eat.'

Charley read this effusion to us at Drury
Lane, and, what is more to the point, paid
the poetical milkman's score at once.

CHARLEY IN COURT (Portugal-street),
before Mr. Commissioner Fonblanque.—
Comical, ever-fresh Mathews appeared in

this debtor's court rather too frequently to be pleasant to his creditors, but generally escaped scot-free. Fonblanque, on one occasion, addressed the comedian as follows:

'With deep regret, Mr. Mathews, I see you in this court again.'

Charley replied, 'Our regrets are mutual, your honour, and would to me be unbearable, only I always have the pleasure of meeting you,' with a graceful bow.

There was a titter in court; and smiling, the learned commissioner allowed Charley to pass through at a shilling in the pound. Nothing like confidence in yourself.

CHARLEY AT DRURY LANE.—A farce called 'No Collusion,' written to ridicule Anderson, the Wizard of the North, the well-known conjuror, at that time manager of Covent Garden, in opposition to Old Drury. The farce abounded with tricks; these, added to Mathews's excellent imitation of the Wizard's voice, manner and dress, formed a capital vehicle for fun and laughter. Previously to its commencement, every evening Charles came before the act drop, hanging a shabby gingham umbrella on a line that extended across the stage attached to the proscenium, with an air of gravity requesting the audience to watch his umbrella, much depended upon that. This rendered the wondering public very attentive to his injunction, constantly gazing at it. Curtain down after juggling feats and ' no collusion'—real Wizard's constant term—Mathews walked on, taking the gingham down, and blandly smiling, thanked them : ' It was a wet night, and he should want it.' Exit, cool as a cucumber.

MADAME VESTRIS.

MADAME VESTRIS.—Paris, London and Naples bore witness to Vestris's wonderful acquirements. Prima donna at the Grand Opera in three European capitals, singing in Italian and French. She was descended from an Italian family. Her father was the well-known engraver, Bartolozzi. She naturally became a good linguist. After a series of triumphs on the lyric stage, she brought her abilities to the English theatres. No one was ever more popular at Drury Lane and Covent Garden. Her attractive person, perfect voice, and bewitching grace few could resist; to see and hear was to admire. Don Giovanni, her saucy Don, almost made intrigue palatable. Vestris as the 'Don' filled every printseller's window with her faultless arms and legs. In truth, the people were Giovanni mad.

MADAME VESTRIS AND THE SHIRTS.— One of her numerous devotees, Lord J. T——e, through her reckless extravagance came to grief and the bankruptcy court. His solicitor, a member of a well-known firm in Hatton Garden, preparing my lord's schedule, one of the items £100,000, a gift to a female friend—Vestris. 'This was paying pretty well for your whistle, my lord.'

One season she owed to a florist in Covent Garden £300 for floral bouquets. This occurred during her lesseeship of the Olympic. Her career was one of reckless extravagance, regardless who. paid or who lost. Her acting of Lady Teazle and Lydia Languish quite equalled her singing. The Lyceum, the Olympic, and Covent Garden were under her tasteful management, assisted by Planché's pen and Beverley's brush, guided by her own refinement. Pieces, especially of fairy lore, were better placed on these respective stages than ever had been witnessed before. This gifted lady retained her supremacy for half a century unrivalled.

MISS FANNY VINING.

Miss Fanny Vining boasts theatrical

ancestry, being the daughter of Frederick Vining.—This lady, with personal charms to be envied, displayed talent, pathos, and deep feeling in the serious walks of the drama, playing Belvidera, Juliet, Mrs. Haller. Marrying E. J. Davenport, she quitted the English stage to settle in America.

E. J. DAVENPORT.

E. J. DAVENPORT, an excellent American actor, came to England with Mrs. Mowatt, authoress and actress. Davenport possessed great versatility, playing such widely distinct characters as Othello, Benedick, and William in ' Black-Eyed Susan.' By his manly bearing and his good voice and delivery, Davenport obtained, in addition to public approbation, much favourable criticism from our press. He first trod the boards of Old Drury under E. T. Smith's management in 1853, in Charles Reade's drama of 'Gold.' His second engagement was to act Iago to Mr. G. V. Brooke's 'Othello,' Wellborn, Richmond, etc. Davenport married and returned to his native country.

EDMUND KEAN, 1787—1833.

EDMUND KEAN, born 1787, in a court in Gray's-inn-lane, steeped in poverty. This remarkable man's career, traced from boyhood to his grave, would form a romance of real life, far exceeding any fiction. A five-act play, entitled 'Kean,' appeared in Paris, illustrating the tragedian's career. In childhood no parents' watchful care ever blessed this bright-eyed boy. His real father is unknown, but Aaron Kean, a Jew, mimic and ventriloquist, had the credit of Kean's parentage. His mother was Nan Carey, a low, dissolute woman, who acted in travelling shows, and sang in public-houses. Sometimes when drink had deprived her of sense and feeling, she might be heard ballad-singing in the streets; her son being left to chance—the worst of nurses—a waif, a stray, a starveling, cast forth by his unnatural mother to starvation or crime. Did not this terrible schooling affect his whole after life? Compelled to work almost before he could well walk, at seven years of age, an imp dancing with others round the witches' cauldron in 'Macbeth,' at Drury Lane (Macbeth, John Kemble), young Kean, the incarnation of roguery and mischief, placed his leg across their path, and down they tumbled over each other, to the delight of the spectators. Not so with the offended tragedian. No more young devils! They were cut out from that night. Young Kean was cast into the streets again, tumbling, posturing, spouting speeches from Shakespeare in low taverns, or harlequinading at Richardson's Show. Inspired by a restless desire for adventure, he hired himself as cabin boy on board a collier. This he quickly abandoned. His only resting-place was the home of a poor actress, Miss Tidswell, in Vinegar-yard, Drury-lane. 'Aunt Tid,' as this kindly creature called herself, laboured earnestly to reclaim the wayward, restless boy, to instil the little learning that she possessed. The sharp-witted lad eagerly caught up everything that might help him in his struggle for fame—bits of Latin, French, scraps of poetry, all were fish that came to young Edmund's net. For a time a vague report was in circulation that some considerate gentleman, struck by his abilities, had sent him to Eton. Mrs. Clarke, a lady of independent means, did take pity on his forlorn condition, having been impressed by his tragic powers. In her house his wild

erratic temperament received a check for
the first time in his life.   Education
dawned upon him, he saw and profited by
the change from want to opulence, from
coarseness to refinement.   This happy
tate unfortunately was not of long dura-
tion.   A vapid talkative visitor spoke of
the boy's origin in terms that roused his
passionate, headstrong will.   He ran away
from Guildford-street, plunged into his old
ways of recklessness and waywardness ; his
hiding-places being circuses, show booths,
public-houses, where he gave recitals, including imitations of the principal actors of
the day.   His passion at one period was to
become an acrobat.   Fencing and dancing
he was master of.   Aunt Tid's treatment
of this wilful, clever boy had been excellent: step by step, teaching him to declaim,
to learn scenes from ‘ Macbeth,’ ‘ Othello,’
‘ Lear,’ ‘ Richard the Third,’ and then act
them before a glass.   Gloster was always

his favourite; he gave the points and action of this arduous character with wonderful ability, foreshadowing his future greatness. Indomitable purpose supported and urged him on to surmount the disappointments that surrounded his rugged path. At length his name became recognised. Beverley engaged him for his circuit, Durham, Shields, Sunderland, etc., to lead the business. At Sunderland he first met Miss Chambers (an Irish lady), Beverley's leading actress. Report had given this lady a private income, most desirable to Kean, who was receiving only twenty-five shillings a week. She quickly set her cap at poor Edmund, admiring his acting and handsome features. It was the old story : flirtation, admiration, declaration, ending in being asked three times in church, the clerk's 'Amen,' and the immutable hoop of gold. The news of this wedding reached Manager Beverley's ears;

the couple were sent for, and Beverley thus addressed them :

'Kean, you know I like you, but my rules must not be broken. Married folks are not attractive in a play-bill. Single young men draw single lasses; single women, if pretty, turn the heads of all the young fellows. You must go; a fortnight's notice. Good-day.'

They did go. Where? Mrs. Kean's fortune turned out to be a myth. Travelling up and down afoot, in and out of towns, villages, barns, and booths. In due time, two small boys, Howard and Charles, added to their heavy burden. Driven to despair, at Jersey, Kean would have enlisted in a marching regiment; but luckily the governor of the island, who had seen him act 'Lear,' persuaded him to give up all thoughts of such a rash step. Hughes, manager of the Exeter circuit, engaged Mr. and Mrs. Kean. They opened at

Exeter. Fortune, tired of frowning on the sorely-tried strollers, shed a ray of sunshine on them. Dr. Arnold, one of the directors of Drury Lane, being on a visit at Exeter, by chance strolled into the theatre and saw Kean act Octavian, in the 'Mountaineers.' Astonished and delighted by the novelty of an entirely new style of pathos and passion he had never witnessed so ably blended before, when the curtain fell he saw Kean and offered him eight pounds a week and a Shakespearian opening part. Elliston, a few days previously, had made an offer of three pounds a week for the Olympic. Naturally the choice fell upon the patent theatre. After months of cold neglect, hopeless delays, and unfeeling remarks from the Drury Lane company upon his shabby appearance and small stature, in one night all difficulties vanished for ever! With his appearance in Shylock, and the electrical effect it produced, Edmund Kean remained master of the scene. A new life was infused into the old dramas : rapidity of utterance and action displaced pomposity and studied gesture. Nature triumphed over art! This desirable change was brought about by 'the little man with the capes ;' a term of contempt applied to his first visit to Drury Lane, on his arrival from Exeter, wearing a second-hand white great-coat with many capes (the fashion of that day), to conceal his shabby attire.

The following is copied from a manuscript play-bill, written by the famous Edmund Kean, when a stroller, to inaugurate a performance at York :

UNDER PATRONAGE.

Ball Room, Minster-yard,

Thursday Evening, October —, 1811.

MR. KEAN

(late of the Theatres Royal, Haymarket

and Edinburgh, and author of 'The Cottage Foundling, or Robbers of Ancona,' now preparing for immediate representation at the Theatre Lyceum), and

Mrs. KEAN

(late of the Theatres Cheltenham and Birmingham), respectfully inform the inhabitants of York and its vicinity, that they will stop

FOR ONE NIGHT ONLY,

on their way to London ; and present such entertainments that have never failed of giving satisfaction, humbly requesting the support of the public.

Part First.

Scenes from the celebrated comedy of

'THE HONEY MOON ;

or,

HOW TO RULE A WIFE'

DUKE ARANZA . . . *Mr. Kean.*
JULIANA . . . . *Mrs. Kean.*

Favourite comic song, 'Beggars and Ballad Singers,' in which Mr. Kean will display his powers of mimicry in the well-known characters of London beggars.

IMITATIONS

of the London performers, viz. :
Kemble,   Cooke,   Braham,   Incledon,
Munden, Fawcett, and
The Young Roscius.

Part Second.

The African Slave's appeal to Liberty !!!
Scenes from the laughable farce,

'THE WATERMAN ;

or,

THE FIRST OF AUGUST.'

TOM TUG (with the song, 'Did you not hear of a Jolly Young Waterman,' and the pathetic ballad of ' Then farewell, my trim-built Wherry '), *Mr. Kean.*
MISS WILHELMINA   .   . *Mrs. Kean.*

After which, Mr. Kean will sing in character, George Alexander Stevens's description of a

STORM.

Part Third.

Scenes from the popular Drama of

'THE CASTLE SPECTRE.'

EARL OSMOND . . . *Mr. Kean.*
ANGELA . . . . *Mrs. Kean.*

Favourite Comic Song of 'The Cosmetic Doctor;' to conclude with the laughable farce of

'SYLVESTER DAGGERWOOD;

or,

THE DUNSTABLE ACTOR.'

FEMALE AUTHOR . . *Mrs. Kean.*
SYLVESTER DAGGERWOOD . *Mr. Kean.*

(In which he will read the celebrated play-bill, written by G. Colman, Esq., and sing the 'Four-and-twenty Puppet-shows,' originally sung by him at the Theatre Royal, Haymarket.)

Each character to be personated in their appropriate dresses, made by the principal theatrical dressmakers of London, viz., Brooks and Heath, Martin, etc.

Front Seats, 2*s.* 6*d.* ; Back Seats, 1*s.*

Doors to be open at six, and begin at seven, precisely.

Tickets to be had at the Printer's.

FIRST AND SECOND GREEN-ROOMS, Drury Lane.—Privilege accorded to actors of ten pounds per week, the first room ; those under five pounds found themselves in the second. When Kean had made the hit that raised him to the highest standard of popularity, he entered the first. An old strolling companion, Hughes, engaged at Drury, receiving three pounds a week, did not presume to cross the threshold of number one. Kean, waiting to go on in

'Richard,' saw him pass one evening, and called to him :

'Dick, I want to speak to you.'

'Beg pardon, sir, I cannot enter the room.'

'What do you mean?'

HUGHES: 'I'm only a three-pounder; they are all tenners that are allowed to sit in the first green-room.'

Kean sent for Rae, and insisted that his old friend should enter. The stage-manager hesitated; it was a rule.

'Well, then,' said the great tragedian, 'you'll play "Richard" to-night without "Gloster."'

This settled a vexed question, once and for all time.

RAE, STAGE-MANAGER OF DRURY LANE, tragedian. Previous to Edmund Kean's advent, Rae played leading parts. The little stroller thrust him from his throne. Richard had to descend to Richmond. With very bad taste Rae had treated

Kean with marked indifference during the rehearsals for 'Shylock.' This Kean never forgot or pardoned. When the astounding success came, Rae's conduct changed towards the despised actor. All now was compliment and polite attention. At a rehearsal of 'Richard the Third'—GLOSTER, *Kean;* RICHMOND, *Rae*—trying their fight for 'Bosworth Field,' Rae asked where he wished Richmond to hit him?

'KEAN (*a master of fence*) : 'Where you can, sir.'

The fight assumed an aspect of reality ; Richard drove Richmond into a corner of the stage, and would not be hit, parried every attempt, laughing at the disconcerted manager. Rae left the West for the East, Old Royalty Theatre, Goodman's Fields. Kean, though still hating him, took a box on Rae's first night, when he appeared as Sir Edward Mortimer in the 'Iron

Chest' (rather magnanimous conduct on the part of the little man with the capes).

EDMUND KEAN, previous to his appearing at Drury Lane, acted 'utility' at the Haymarket for thirty shillings per week.

EDMUND KEAN AT EXETER. — Mrs. Bartley starring in Lady Macbeth, Hughes, the leading actor, was suddenly taken ill; Kean, who was then playing second parts, took Macbeth in the Banquet scene. Whenever a star appeared the manager furnished his guests with bread-and-cheese, placed on the tinselled plates. Lady Macbeth, as hostess, bade all her Thanes welcome, wishing graciously that good digestion might await on appetite.

KEAN (*aside to his brother actors*): 'Eat, eat, you vagabonds—eat your fill; it is not often that you get "star" bread.'

EDMUND KEAN AND OXBERRY.

CRAVEN'S HEAD TAVERN, Drury-lane, William Oxberry, a Drury Lane comedian, was the host. Edmund Kean loved a social glass, and never forgot old companions of his former wanderings. Star now of the dramatic hemisphere, he still indulged in his former habits. Oxberry held a musical club at his tavern weekly, at which Edmund Kean presided. A club-night happened to fall upon a 'Richard the Third' night at Drury. 'What's to be done?' thought Oxberry; 'the chair will be vacant.' Visitors were wont to crowd the Craven's Head to look at the town's wonder, Kean—a thing to remember and talk about—especially for those who were privileged to hear him sing. 'The Jolly Dogs' (our clubbites' name) became as difficult to enter as the 'Carlton' or 'United Service' of our day.

OXBERRY: 'Ned, you'll never be able to take the chair to-night in time.'

'Won't I, Billy? For a dinner and a bottle of port, I am there.'

The wager was accepted by Billy, Kean acted Gloster very quickly, and in his fight, a great feature, whispered to Wallack (who played Richmond) :

'Kill me quickly to-night, I'm due at the "Jolly Dogs."'

The curtain down, wrapped in a great-coat, rapidly he ran down the Lane, jumping into the chair a few minutes before the club opened, amidst thunders of applause. There sat the last 'Plantagenet' in the habit as he lived (Kean had not taken off his Richard's dress), won his wager, and filled Billy's till that evening to repletion.

Kean acting at Richmond a night with Klanert, shared half the house, £40. This he spent after the performance of 'Othello,' with a set of boon companions from London,—supper, wine, and loo. He wrote to his friend Klanert from the 'Star and Garter,' thus :

'DEAR KLANERT,

'All my cash gone; I'm in pawn for ten pounds; take me out. Send cheque or money by waiter,

'Yours,

'E. KEAN.'

JOHN KEMBLE AND EDMUND KEAN.— Kemble would never see Kean or any of his performances at Drury Lane at the time he was drawing all London by his extraordinary genius. Cribb, the picture-dealer of King-street, frequently pressed Kemble to give his opinion of the new star. At length the last of the Romans did unbend. Cribb sent him a box for Drury on one of Kean's Othello nights. Anxious to hear what Kemble would say about it, he stopped him in the street, with :

'Well, you did see the little man, Kean, eh ?' laughing.

'No, sir, I did not see Mr. Kean, I

saw Othello; and further, I shall never act the part again.'

And with a tragedy stride, he left the delighted picture-dealer rubbing his hands in great glee.

KEAN, driven from the London stage by the powerfully written articles that daily appeared in the *Times* in connexion with his *crim. con.* case, Alderman Cox *v.* Edmund Kean, resolved to go to America. On his way, he played one night at Liverpool—'Richard the Third'—previous to embarking. Part of the audience hissed him in every scene—others applauded. Greatly enraged, the tragedian at the conclusion of the play strode before the curtain, and spoke as follows:

'Ladies and gentlemen,—I thank those that applauded me. As for the others, I have only this to say to them, let them find a better actor if they can. Goodnight.'

Edmund Kean, 1814, at Drury Lane.
—The following was one of the early an-
nouncements of his appearance:

'Drury Lane Theatre, February 7th,
1814, Shakespeare's play of "The Merchant of Venice." Shylock, Mr. Kean.
Mr. Kean, who has four times performed
the part of Shylock with increasing attraction and the unanimous plaudits of overflowing audiences, will repeat the character
to-morrow and Thursday.

'Saturday, February 12th, will be performed for the first time at this theatre
Shakespeare's tragedy of "Richard the
Third," with new scenes, dresses, and decorations.

'Richard, *Mr. Kean* (his first appearance
in that character).'

Kean's last appearance on the London
stage was on March 25, 1833, at the
Theatre Royal, Covent Garden. The play
was 'Othello.' Othello, *Mr. Kean;* Iago,

Mr. Charles Kean. In the third act, Kean, worn out by illness, whispered to his son, falling on his shoulder, 'Charles, I am dying! He was led from the stage, never to return. Kean died May 15, 1833, aged 46, and was buried at Richmond, Surrey. He expired in the Theatre House (his residence) on the Green.

'It is a vulgar error to call Mr. Kean's acting undignified. It is exactly like calling the 'Beggar's Opera' vulgar. They must have strange notions of dignity, even in the most commonplace sense of the term, who do not find it in Mr. Kean's manner of dismissing Cassio from his command:

> "I love thee, Cassio,
> But never more be officer of mine."

He is quite dignified enough for Shakespeare, which is all that can be reasonably demanded of him. Sir Giles Overreach, if not the greatest, is certainly the most

perfect of all Mr. Kean's performances.
It is quite faultless.   The last act without
doubt is the most terrific exhibition of
human passion that has been witnessed on
the modern stage—for conception and execution it cannot be surpassed. "Othello"
was without comparison the noblest exhibition of human genius we ever witnessed :
the performance was worthy to have taken
place in Shakespeare's own age—with
himself—he and Fletcher, Ford, Spenser,
and Sidney for an audience. We cannot
help fancying how they would have gone
into the green-room, perhaps—Shakespeare, we are sure, would—and with a
smiling yet serious and earnest delight
upon their faces, have held out their hands,
and thanked him. Think of a shake of
the hand from Shakespeare, and of de-
serving it too.'—*Blackwood's Magazine,*
1818.

CHARLES KEAN, 1811—1868.

CHARLES KEAN, son of Edmund Kean, was born in 1811, and educated at Eton. He was intended by his father for the East India Company's service, a cadetship having been presented to the elder Kean by a director. This appointment Charles refused, wishing to remain with his mother; an excellent, thoughtful son, supplying her comforts, administering to her sorrows. Bunn, a keen appreciator of a 'name, offered Charles Kean twelve pounds a week to appear a certain number of nights at Drury Lane. He made his bow to a crowded house, Tuesday, October 2, 1827, in Home's play of ' Douglas.'

CAST.

LORD RANDOLPH, *Mr. Mude.*
OLD NORVAL, *Mr. Cooper.*
GLENALVON, *Mr. James Wallack.*

Young Norval, *Mr. Kean, junior* (his first
appearance on any stage).
Lady Randolph, *Mrs. W. West.*
Anne, *Mrs. Knight.*

His *début* was greeted with brilliant and
unanimous approbation. His next character, Frederick in 'Lovers' Vows,'
followed by Achmet in 'Barbarossa.'
Twenty-four nights terminated this his first
engagement. He now wisely sought practice in provincial towns, returning to Drury
Lane to play 'Hamlet.' This proved a
hit. He repeated the part for eighty
nights in one season, and was highly commended by the press and public. Miss
Burdett Coutts, by her patronage, largely
assisted the young actor's progress. Offers
now multiplied; and all managers were
eager to have the new star. Perseverance,
gentlemanly conduct, excellent taste, raised
Charles Kean to a foremost rank in his art.
Marrying Miss Ellen Tree, with this clever

lady's skill and talent (no small aid) he ventured upon management at the Princess's Theatre. Here for ten years he produced plays, dramas, burlesques, and pantomimes, in the best and most complete style, no expense nor pains being spared to give effect, especially to his Shakespearian revivals. They were perfect. The last play produced under his excellent direction was ' The Tempest.' A tour to America and Australia added largely to his fame and gains. He died at the early age of fifty-six, and the theatrical profession lost a kind considerate friend and liberal manager.

Testimonial and dinner given to Charles Kean, 1855, at St. James's Hall, by his old Eton school-fellows—Duke of Newcastle, Mr. Gladstone, Mr. Goschen, the Earl of Carlisle, Sir John Burgoyne, Mr. Walpole, Mr. Pickersgill, Mr. Millais, Mr. Stone, etc., his friends and the public, in token of their estimation of Charles Kean's

public and private character. The presence
of more than eight hundred gentlemen bore
testimony to this. Mr. Gladstone, in a
capital speech, eulogised his old 'form-
fellow' and captain of their boat—Kean.
The Duke of Newcastle coupled with his
health praise for his unremitting exertions
to raise the stage by his exposition of our
great dramatist Shakespeare; alluding to
the production of his plays so admirably
placed on the Princess's boards by Kean,
and the influence that a well-governed
theatre must perforce exercise on the minds
of the people. Addressing Kean as his
honoured friend, the Duke, in the name of
the subscribers, presented to him a superb
silver épergne valued at £1,000. This
substantial gift was supplemented with an
address on vellum, expressing their pleasur-
able feelings. Kean's reply embraced many
topics, not omitting his wife's zealous co-
operation with himself in their good work

to encourage morality and render the stage a school for amusement, refinement, and instruction.

CHARLES KEAN AT BRIGHTON, 1856.— The leading actor of the theatre, very studious of his dignity, annoyed at Kean's casting him in secondary characters (a custom with 'stars'), chose to treat his rehearsals with negligence, pooh-poohing instruction. Kean, always anxious for his performances going well, took considerable pains in imparting his views. This the ill-bred tyro resisted with :

'Sir, you need not trouble yourself about me; I know the play backwards.'

'Probably you do,' replied Kean ; 'but that is not the way I play it, Mr. ——.'

Silence reigned, except aside-tittering at the crest-fallen actor.

CHARLES KEAN AND HIS MANAGER ELLICE.—When Charles Kean rehearsed an important play, after instructing his company, he usually seated himself in one of the boxes to watch their acting. At a rehearsal of ' Richard the Second,' one of his great revivals, Kean was seated as usual, Ellice on the stage ; performers at work.

KEAN (*suddenly*) : 'Stop, stop, Ellice! push that back' (*pointing to a wing*).

His manager, mistaking, pushed a chorus gentleman back.

' No, no, Ellice ; I meant the wing. Wings are wood and canvas, not flesh and blood. Ellice, you are an ass !'

' Yes, sir ' (*bowing to Kean*).

· ' Don't answer me, sir ; you know you are, to mistake carpenters' work for a man.'

CHARLES KEAN AND HIS MOTHER.—Mrs. Kean thought her Charles was the best actor living or dead. This opinion she sought to impress on all visitors and friends. Kean, giving a dinner-party to some distinguished guests, begged his mother to abstain from her usual encomiums at the table. This was promised; but Charles, to make all sure, arranged that if by chance she forgot, he would touch his shirt-collar to remind her. Dinner served, a noble lord seated next Mrs. Kean, they discussed topics of the day, politics, etc. Macready's acting in ' Richelieu,' his lordship highly praised. This Mrs. K. could not allow.

' My Charles is '——— shirt-collar touched —pause.

My Lord : ' Yes.'

Mrs. K. : ' Is the best '——— collar raised an inch—another pause.

' Beg pardon,' from the nobleman.

' Well then, my Charles is the best actor that ever trod. There, it's out, Charles ; it's no use pulling your collar up to your eyes.'

Kean's feelings can be imagined.

Charles Kean on Letter-writing.— Breakfasting once with Kean at Bath, he

had occasion to open his desk.   I remarked
on the precise and orderly way in which
his letters were labelled and kept.

'Yes,' replied Kean, 'I am very particular about letters, never write more than
compelled; they are so apt to reappear
when not wanted.'

Quite true!   Read, for example, the
Divorce Court reports of our day.

I wrote a little drama for Mrs. Kean,
which was accepted for the Princess's.

> 'Tavistock Square,
>
> 'June 4, 1854.
>
> 'Dear Sir,
>
> 'If you will call at the Theatre
> Princess's, Captain Cole will arrange with
> you for your drama, "The Gambler's Wife:"
> my wife likes the part.
>
> 'Yours truly,
>
> 'Charles Kean.

E. Stirling, Esq.,
    'T. R. D. Lane.'

MRS. CHARLES KEAN (ELLEN TREE),
1806—1880.

ELLEN TREE (Mrs. Charles Kean), born 1806, branch of a prolific Tree (*père* Tree), first came out in public at Drury Lane, with her sister Anne. I acted with Miss Ellen at Ware, in Hertfordshire—a place boasting a bed of such dimensions as to hold six couples, and called the 'Great Bed of Ware'—at a temporary theatre, under Manager Bullen—Inn Assembly-room. Bullen, his better half, and a numerous assembly of olive-branches, contrived to live, migrating from town to town, and leading a gipsy life : minus green lanes, heather and gorse, commons and wild freedom—only known to the Romanees. In our very original theatre the scenes were of calico, bedaubed, not painted. The stage was raised by borrowing deal planks and placing them on the floor.

The lights were oil lamps, the curtain was painted on linen. Three scenes represented everything possible and impossible. Tables and chairs, etc., were loaned from friendly shop-keepers. LADY SNEERWELL, *Mrs. Bullen*, attired in satin, white feathers, etc., took the money at the doors (a narrow passage). Wise receiver! LADY TEAZLE, *Ellen Tree.* CHARLES SURFACE, *Edward Stirling*. All the rest were Bullens. In the screen scene, when Lady Teazle is revealed to the gaze of her astonished husband, the stage was so small that the screen (a clothes-horse) fell on the lamps, extinguishing them. Sir Peter (Bullen), and Lady Sneerwell (Mrs. B.) soon put that to rights by relighting. Our receipts for nightly performances, twelve pounds ten shillings and sixpence.

The following letter refers to a little piece of mine, about which some difficulty presented itself in arranging the cast :

'Tavistock Square,

'September 6th, 1856.

'Dear Mr. Stirling,

'We have read your pretty poetical little piece and like it much. Charles will have it. Please forward terms. But who is to do the cobbler? Frank Mathews's style is too hard. This is a puzzle; perhaps you will think of someone.

'Yours truly,

'Ellen Kean.

'E. Stirling Esq.,

'T. R. Drury Lane.'

The death of this amiable and accomplished lady took place as these records were being finally prepared for press. She died on Saturday, August 21st, 1880, at the age of seventy-four, full of years and honours.

WILLIAM OXBERRY.

William Oxberry. — Player, author, editor of an excellent edition of plays bearing his name, and licensed victualler. Here was occupation sufficient for one man. Many years a member of Drury Lane companies, a special favourite with the play-going public, Oxberry's journey through life might be considered a happy one. Varied were his talents, and well-used by managers. Our comedian played all and everything. Few bills that did not announce William Oxberry's appearance. Justice Greedy, Dr. Cantwell, Mawworm, Sulky, Goldfinch, Sir Toby Belch, Touchstone, · were a few of this clever comedian's personations. He died at his house, ' The Craven's Head,' Drury Lane.

SHERWIN.

SHERWIN. — A sound good actor, in countrymen highly respectable ; always acting with judgment, he pleased, and held his position in Drury Lane for many years.

WILLIAM BENNETT.

WILLIAM BENNETT, a very useful actor, frequently a double to more eminent performers, Munden, Dowton, Bartley, etc. Bennett, always perfect and respectable in what he did, kept his ground on the boards of Drury for forty years, and became a household word, being familiarly known as ' Billy Bennett ' with the frequenters of the theatre and her Majesty's servants.

MRS. NESBITT (LADY BOOTHBY).

MRS. NESBITT (afterwards Lady Boothby) —This charming actress was born of a noble family ; the carelessness and extravagance of her father compelled her, however, together with her sisters, to seek their living on the stage, first in small towns, villages, etc.—a precarious mode of bringing up his beautiful girls. The gallant father, once in her Majesty's service, resembled a certain Costigan, well known to fame, and to readers of Thackeray. After many weary pilgrimages under her theatrical name of Miss Mordaunt, Alexander Lee engaged her for Drury Lane. To be once seen was for her to conquer. She rapidly won the admiration of her audiences and a husband, Captain Nesbitt of the Guards, unfortunately killed a few months after their marriage at a steeplechase. Our pretty widow, now a first-rate artiste and attraction, passed from house to house, always drawing and filling treasuries, when acting in her best parts of Rosalind, Lady Teazle, Lady Gay Spanker, Constance. Who that ever heard her merry laugh at Neighbour Wildrake's stupidity can forget it? Her second matrimonial venture was a curious one, and remains a puzzle to this day. Sir William Boothby had neither the attractions of wealth nor of youth. Perhaps it was the title that she coveted. This brilliant woman died at an early age, much regretted by all true lovers of art and genuine acting.

JOHN VANDENHOFF, 1790—1861.

J. VANDENHOFF (born 1790).—An actor of sound judgment. All he undertook was well done. Never rising to genius, Vandenhoff was far above mediocrity. The Liverpool public would not hear of a rival to their local favourite. I engaged Vandenhoff and his clever daughter for Covent Garden to act in 'Antigone' and a new play by Spicer called 'Honesty.' Vanden hoff's 'Creon,' and Miss Vandenhoff's 'Antigone,' on this resuscitation of Sophocles' great tragedy, proved eminently acceptable and gratifying to literary men, scholars, and public. Vandenhoff acted for years at Drury Lane, until his daughter died. This domestic loss, sorely felt by a loving parent, hastened his retirement from the stage, and he subsided into private life, honoured and respected.

MRS. MARDYN.

MRS. MARDYN AND LORD BYRON (Drury Lane).—Byron, always partial to actors, and still more to actresses, usually during rehearsals lounged in the green room, chatting to the performers. One very wet day, a pretty actress, Mrs. Mardyn, lamenting her disappointment at not being able to hire a hackney-coach, residing as she did at a considerable distance from the theatre, Byron instantly placed at her disposal his carriage which was standing at the stage-door. Joyfully Mrs. Mardyn drove home in his lordship's chariot ; not quite so joyfully did poor Byron receive his greeting on his arrival home. His wife, Lady Byron, a woman whose temper was at the best of times none of the sweetest, was in high dudgeon when she heard of an actress using *her* carriage.

This seemingly trifling occurrence had its share in leading to the separation that soon after followed.

MISS O'NEILL (LADY BECHER), BORN 1791.

MISS O'NEILL (Lady Becher), born 1791, one of the most natural of actresses that the stage ever possessed. Of Irish birth, this refined artist first played at the Crow-street Theatre, Dublin. Her attraction proved so great that an offer for Covent Garden speedily came in 1814. Here she appeared in Juliet, always her best part, October 6. Her modest lady-like demeanour, and deep impassioned feeling, created an impression never to be eradicated. After a short season at Drury Lane, our Irish Siddons bade England adieu to marry Mr., afterwards Sir William Becher, retiring with the good wishes and regrets of thousands. Her last performance at Drury Lane took place July, 1818, in the character of Mrs. Haller in 'The Stranger.'

JAMES WALLACK, 1791—1864.

JAMES WALLACK (known as 'handsome Jem' among his theatrical brethren).— Assuredly a smart fellow in the London world's estimation, Wallack never reached leading tragedy. His *rôle* was seconds, high comedy, and that which he most excelled in, melodrama. His interpretation of romantic heroes won all praise. For example, in 'The Brigand' he sang with taste a ballad, 'Gentle Zitella,' accompanying himself on the guitar. This effort turned the heads of the young lady frequenters of Drury Lane—query, did the old ones escape this infection? 'Don Cæsar de Bazan'—the career of this Spanish scamp was made attractive by Wallack, who also played Richard in Soane's now-forgotten drama, 'The Innkeeper's Daughter,' a fine piece of acting ; Martin in Jerrold's 'Rent Day,' a home picture, truthful and realistic. Wallack acted

Richmond, Cassio, Iago, Captain Absolute, well. His attempting Macbeth and Shylock was a mistake. He was a great favourite in America, and quitted the London stage to settle there, establishing a first-rate theatre, called 'Wallack's.' At his death the theatre became the property of his son, Leslie Wallack, and continues to be one of the best conducted in the United States, ranking deservedly high with the more cultured part of the community.

MONTAGUE STANLEY.

MONTAGUE STANLEY appeared in 'Romeo' at Drury Lane, and was well received. In Edinburgh Stanley was a great favourite. His character was irreproachable, and his manners elegant. He had a considerable taste for painting, and his pictures realised good prices in 'Auld Reekie.'

WILLIAM HENRY WEST BETTY (BORN 1792).

MASTER HENRY BETTY.—This renowned juvenile actor first appeared at Covent Garden, December 1, 1804. Very handsome, highly intellectual, well tutored by his father, a doctor, Master Betty made a fortune before others began to earn their bread. He became the rage of the town, the idol of the fair—admired by men and women alike. In fact, this extraordinary boy usurped all attention for a period; the public deserted all their old favourites for this new one. The Kembles, even Mrs. Siddons, were eclipsed by this boyish star's attraction. It is indeed amusing to observe to what extent a popular mania of this kind will lead. Dozens of carriages were in waiting nightly, after Betty's performances, to carry him off: fierce was the struggle between the *élite* of female society which should have this new toy to lionise in their *salons;* grave lawyers, statesmen, poets, critics, were each and all delighted with the graceful boy's precocious talents. People gained admission to the theatre with the greatest difficulty, the crowding became so great—fainting, screaming, fighting, to get a peep at the prodigy. Opinion was divided among the judges of acting; some elected Betty before Garrick; all agreed that he was superior to Kemble. Large sums of money came into the treasury and into the pockets of Dr. Betty, who foolishly lost a considerable portion of it in extravagance and the gaming-table; fortunately, sufficient had been settled on the boy by his mother to provide a good income for life. His theatrical popularity soon began to wane; the novelty had worn off, and when Betty re-appeared at Drury Lane as an adult, his attraction was found to have passed away, and the houses were indifferently attended. He lived to a good old age, in domestic comfort, cheered by the companionship of a loving wife and a dutiful son.

Jeu-d'esprit on precocious children's acting, directed to Master Betty's performances :

'On Monday next will be presented

"THE TEMPEST,"

in which, by particular desire, the part of Caliban will be performed for her own benefit by

MISS BIDDY SUCKLING,

an infant, not yet quite four years old! and who appeared in the same character, *almost two years ago*, with such universal applause at the

THEATRE ROYAL, DUBLIN.

'N.B.—The Infant Caliban will introduce, for that night only, a song in character and accompanied by herself, to which will be added

"LOVE À LA MODE."

The part of Sir Archy Mac Sarcasm by the child.

' N.B.—The parts of Coriolanus, King Henry the Eighth, and Shylock, have been some time in rehearsal by Miss Biddy, and will be performed by her as soon as the daily *Bulletin* shall declare her sufficiently recovered from her hooping-cough—a dis-order which the public must have perceived is rather friendly than otherwise to her performance of Caliban, in which she will therefore continue during the remainder of the season. The pet will as usual be led into the boxes every night of Miss Biddy's appearance in Caliban.

' The manager further respectfully acquaints the public, that in consequence of the immense damage and calamitous accidents which have arisen from the unex-ampled pressure of the crowd on the child's nights, skilful surgeons will henceforth be regularly stationed in all parts of the house.

' *Vivant Rex et Regina.*'

ARCHER.

ARCHER, a member of the Drury Lane company, under Elliston's *régime*, had a very lax way of not acquiring the words of his varied round of characters, trusting to memory, or more frequently to chance. Archer, with fair abilities, made little way. Playing Appius Claudius in 'Virginius,' with his usual carelessness, seated in the forum, a book placed under one of the gas burners at the wing enabling him to read, one of his companions wickedly turned the book upside down. Archer began with sonorous declamation addressing the assembled Roman people, faltered for a word, cast his eyes on the book, and perceived at once the joke that had been perpetrated. A long pause ensued. Appius Claudius had vanished from his memory. Cato came to the rescue. Deliberately he recited to the astonished plebeians Cato's celebrated soliloquy, commencing ' It must be so—Plato, thou reasonest well,' to the end of the speech : ' I'm weary of conjectures ; this must end 'em. Lictors, follow me. Claudius [his client], I'll hear more of this case to-morrow ' (strutting off the stage pompously in Roman fashion).

WILLIAM CHARLES MACREADY, BORN 1793.

WILLIAM MACREADY was born in 1793, of Irish parentage. Macready's father managed the Bristol and Birmingham Theatres, and played in London a season or two at Covent Garden. His wish was that his son should become a Catholic priest. Adverse circumstances, the failure of his father, and a second marriage, induced Macready to try the stage, much against his father's wish. The attempt made, several years passed before Macready conquered ; his excessively nervous temperament, retiring habits, and reserved manners created an ill-feeling among those actors who did not understand him. Naturally a generous, kind man, he had the reputation of being overbearing and tyrannical. He appeared at Covent Garden as Orestes, and remained with the Kembles some seasons, gradually rising in his art. Time at last rewarded his study and application ; he became an actor of the highest grade, rivalling the Kembles, Kean, Young, etc., in characters that he had made his own. Werner in Lord Byron's play, William Tell, Virginius. Richelieu, Evelyn in ' Money,' Claude Melnotte, etc. His Shakespearian personations were admirable : Hotspur, Macbeth, Othello, Iago, Richard the Second. Macready's home life was one of exceeding happiness, with a wife, an actress (Miss Atkins), whom he devotedly loved, a family of rare talents, and the society of the most distinguished men of the day. His fortune was realised by constant labour. All his ventures were profitable but one, viz., the management of Drury Lane; there he lost time and money. I gave him fifty pounds a night for six weeks at the Surrey Theatre, his first appearance on a minor stage. Macready retired in the full vigour of his health and power. Macbeth was his final performance. Living to a good old age, he died at Cheltenham, honoured and respected.

MRS. W. WEST.

MRS. W. WEST (Miss Cooke), born at Bath, an actress of moderate capacity, good-looking, and of fine appearance. Unfortunately for her career at Drury, she followed Rae's example, neglecting Kean's rehearsals and scornfully objecting to his requests relative to stage business. When power came into the snubbed actor's grasp, he in turn scorned Mrs. W. West, objecting to act with her. This threw her out of the cast in all important plays, leaving her in the cold shade.

MRS. BLAND.

MRS. BLAND, 1810, vocalist and actress, very much liked at Drury Lane under Elliston's management. Her ballads were always an attraction in the bills. She frequently sang between the play and the farce. Old English music and clear utterance of words, without the redundance of modern ornament—too frequently spoiling melody. 'Sally in our Alley,' sung by Mrs. Bland, never failed to move her audience to tears by its truthful feeling and execution, a true triumph of artistic skill.

LAPORTE.

LAPORTE, a French comedian of high repute, tried the effect of his talents on a Metropolitan audience at Drury Lane, playing Sosia in Plautus's comedy of 'Amphitryon.' Laporte's French accent militated somewhat against permanent success. An English piece, 'The Lottery Ticket,' gave the comedian a better chance of being appreciated. His acting of the plotting little village lawyer, Wormwood, was greatly relished at the time.

MISS SMITHSON.

MISS SMITHSON, a young actress of ability, never gained a high position at Drury Lane: it was reserved for a French audience to discover her talent. When Macready took an English company to Paris, Miss Smithson was his leading lady. She vastly pleased the Parisians by her natural acting and handsome appearance; in fact, she was the attraction rather than Macready himself.

MRS. BUNN (MISS SOMERVILLE).

MRS. BUNN (Miss Somerville).—Leading lady at Drury Lane, during her husband's lesseeship. In the leading *rôle* of tragedy this lady excelled: Lady Macbeth, Constance, Elvira, Helen Macgregor, and Portia. As Queen Elizabeth in Scott's 'Kenilworth,' dramatised by Bunn, her stately figure and fine acting greatly added to the spectacular drama's success.

Miss Philips appeared in Juliet, and was well received. She continued at 'Drury' for several seasons, playing juvenile tragedy and comedy.

Miss Brothers came out as Portia, successfully. Mrs. Ogilvie, Miss Dance, Miss Lydia Kelly, Miss Lacy, Miss Povey, were all highly efficient in their different grades, but never achieved a leading rank.

ROBERT KEELEY, 1794—1869.

Robert Keeley, first a printer, secondly a player, began theatrical life in a strolling community of 'Rogues and Vagabonds.'[*] Master Keeley's troop playing in a barn or outhouse, near Highgate, the low comedian (Keeley) singing a comic song between the

---

[*] *Vide* an edict of Edward III. directing them to be whipped from town to tything if found loitering or playing in their lewd interludes. This enlightened act of a wise king remained unrepealed for 500 years.

acts (which was customary then), just at a refrain,

'Mr. Thumpum, the drummer, so hearty and bold,
                    Rub-a-dub !
Went to visit his sweetheart, Moll Cook, I've been told,
                    Rub-a-dub !
When he went to the area and softly cried hist !
He slily slipp'd down, they met, and they kiss'd,
When she slapp'd the best part of a goose in his fist,
    With a rub-a-dub oh ! row di dow !'

down, to the roll of the drum, came the roof on the astonished singer and audience, followed by screams, cries, and clouds of dust, plaster, and bricks. Everyone fled in consternation. The hopes of the manager crushed, the season finished, no more 'rub-a-dubs' until further notice for poor Bob Keeley ; consequently no money on Saturday for Rub-a-dub. He marched out of Highgate chap-fallen.

MRS. KEELEY (MARY GOWARD), born 1806.

MRS. KEELEY (Mary Goward), born at Ipswich, in 1806, first made her curtsey to a Metropolitan audience at the old English

Opera House (Lyceum). Under the fostering care of Mr. Arnold, manager, she made quick progress ; her singing was as much admired as her natural acting. Keeley, a member of the company, speedily sang himself into Mary Goward's good graces ; she accepted his hand and name. Much prized by playgoers, constantly engaged, the serio-comic couple amassed money. Trip to America, Drury Lane, Covent Garden, Haymarket ; last, not least, the management of the Lyceum. This proved a silver mine to the Keeleys. Many of Mrs. Keeley's best characters were seen at the Adelphi ; notably Smike and Jack Sheppard. When Fanny Kelly retired, Mrs. Keeley filled her place, astonishing the public by her pathos and sympathetic acting in serious parts. Living in competence, this clever actress, happy in her domestic circle, bade dull care farewell.

JUNIUS BRUTUS BOOTH, 1796—1852.

JUNIUS BRUTUS BOOTH, an actor of

great ability, engaged by John Kemble to oppose Edmund Kean, the absorbing star of old Drury Lane; filling the house nightly by the force of genius; discounting Kemble at Covent Garden. In style, stature, and acting, Booth greatly resembled Kean. He appeared February 12th, 1817, in 'Richard the Third.' The impression that he made on the public was most favourable, despite strong opposition of the 'Wolf Club,' Keanites, etc. A contest arose by the Drury Lane Committee claiming his services (Booth had been in treaty with both houses). This gave his opponents a chance of annoying him. They did so, refusing to listen to him on his third appearance. The management issued the following notice :—

'Thursday, Feb. 27th, 1817.

'MR. BOOTH,

last Tuesday, made his third appearance at this theatre in the character of

'KING RICHARD THE THIRD.

After repeated attempts to give an explanation to the audience, and implore them not to suffer an humble individual to be made the victim of disputes between the two theatres, no hearing was allowed him; but as far as the proprietors could judge from the cheering at the dropping of the curtain, a vast majority was in favour of Mr. Booth. He will therefore perform " Richard " again on Saturday next, and throws himself on the mercy and liberality of Englishmen.'

At the expiration of the Covent Garden season, and tempted by a large salary, he quitted the theatre for Drury Lane, to act with Kean — a wrong step. The rival tragedians appeared on the stage of Old Drury, — ' Othello' the play — *Othello*, KEAN; *Iago*, BOOTH. The result, triumph of the Moor over his Ancient. Booth left Drury Lane, to act at the Coburg and

Royalty Theatres ; ultimately left England for America. There he won fame and fortune most deservedly. If Kean had not appeared before him, Booth would have been the actor of that day.

PAUL BEDFORD, 1798—1869.

PAUL BEDFORD, 1826.—His first wife, Miss Green, appeared at Drury Lane, in the Ballad Opera of ' Love in a Village.' HAWTHORN, *Paul ;* ROSETTA, *Miss Green.* Bedford then sang well, and had a fine appearance and jovial spirits. His wife being graceful and a good vocalist, proved an acquisition to the London stage. The handsome couple remained at Drury Lane during Elliston's lessecship. Paul then migrated to Vauxhall Gardens. I engaged him from there for the Adelphi.

BENJAMIN WEBSTER (BORN 1798).

BENJAMIN WEBSTER, manager, author, actor, the Nestor of the stage, was born at Bath, September 3, 1798. This well-known man filled a large portion of theatrical life for nearly sixty years. He first appeared at Drury Lane in the year 1826. No one in his time played so many parts. A fair musician, a graceful dancer (his father was a professor of dancing at Bath), Webster's early career, like that of many of his brethren, was beset with trouble and privation. His first engagement at Drury was to play utility and second Harlequin in pantomime. Luckily for young Webster, a small character-part fell to his share, in a new version of 'Gil Blas'—*Gil Blas*, Miss Kelly ; *Captain Rolando*, Wallack ; a gouty negro, *Dominique*, Webster. This opportunity afforded him a chance to rise ; he played it admirably. His talent was recognised by Elliston, and rewarded, the part of Humphrey Dobbins in Colman's comedy, ' The Poor Gentleman,' being next assigned to him. Cast very fine.

'POOR GENTLEMAN,' 1829.

SIR CHARLES CROPLAND, *Mr. Hooper.*

FREDERICK, *Jones.*

SIR ROBERT BRAMBLE, *Dowton.*

LIEUT. WORTHINGTON, *Cooper.*

OLLAPOD, *Mathews.*

CORPORAL FROSS, *Liston.*

STEPHEN HARROWBY, *Harley.*

FARMER HARROWBY, *Sherwin.*

HUMPHREY DOBBINS, *Webster.*

EMILY WORTHINGTON, *Miss Ellen Tree.*

MISS MACTAB, *Mrs. Davison.*

DAME HARROWBY, *Mrs. Harlowe.*

A solo entertainment was given by Webster, at the Strand, when it first opened (originally Burford's Panorama), entitled 'Webster's Wallet of Whim and Waggery.' This followed the elder Mathews's entertainments very closely. Our comedian now found himself ensconced at the snug little Haymarket Theatre, engaged by Morris, proprietor (*ci-devant* footman).

This proved a fortunate step for Webster ; he remained playing doubles for Liston, Dowton, W. Farren, and original first-rate parts for himself for many years, until the death of his patron, Morris, placed the management in his own hands. Webster conducted the theatre with judgment and liberality, employing the best actors and actresses, and writers of the highest class, such as Sheridan Knowles, Sir Edward Bulwer Lytton, Poole, Planché, Buckstone, Bernard, Morton, etc. Among the many works he produced were ' Money,' ' The Sea-Captain,' ' The Love-Chase,' ' Richelieu in Love,' etc. All the best performers from time to time graced the little Haymarket stage, retiring from it with reputation and large profit. In 1844, Webster and Madame Celeste took the Adelphi. Their joint management went merrily on ; novelties followed in quick succession. ' Green Bushes ' (ever to remain green) ;

'Flowers of the Forest,' which brought Buckstone to the fore on his own ground ; 'Janet Pride,' and a score of effective dramas, flowed from Boucicault's pen. The Theatre Royal, Liverpool, the Princess's, the Olympic, were all rented and conducted by Webster and Madame Celeste. Fortune, however, began to change her smiles into frowns. Clouds arose in the theatrical atmosphere, monetary matters not flourishing.

Adelphi rebuilding, Welsh slate-quarries and other matters led to partnership with Chatterton of Drury Lane,—like all such arrangements, commencing with roseate hues, and terminating too frequently in Basinghall-street or separation. A complimentary benefit, at Drury Lane, to Mr. B. Webster, March 2nd, 1874, realised about £1,200. Bill of fare, Sheridan's 'School for Scandal.'

CAST.

SIR PETER TEAZLE, *Mr. Phelps.*

Joseph Surface, *Creswick.*

Charles Surface, *Charles Mathews.*

Sir Benjamin Backbite, *Buckstone.*

Crabtree, *Compton.*

Careless, *H. Montague.*

Trip, *Clarke.*

Moses, *Toole.*

Snake, *Thorne.*

Rowley, *H. Wigan.*

Sir Harry, *W. Santley.*

Sir Toby, *Billington.*

Servants, *David James, Righton.*

Lady Teazle, *Miss Helen Faucit.*

Lady Sneerwell, *Mrs. Mellon.*

Mrs. Candour, *Mrs. Stirling.*

Maria, *Miss F. Bateman.*

Lady Teazle's Maid, *Miss F. Farren.*

Henry Irving

recited 'Eugène Aram.'

Mrs. Keeley

delivered an address, written by Mr. John Oxenford, to which Webster replied, surrounded by the *élite* of his profession, grouped on the stage.

Stage Manager, E. STIRLING.

MRS. WARNER (MISS HUDDART) 1804—1854.

MRS. WARNER (Miss Huddart).—Her parents were actors, and Polly Huddart commenced her labours before she walked or spoke—carried on the stage as an infant in her mother's arms. After partaking all the ups and downs of a provincial wandering life, her father, Charles Huddart, engaged with his clever daughter at the Surrey—the old Surrey, part circus, part theatre—under Tom Dibdin's management. Miss Huddart quickly gained the approbation of her transpontine admirers. Her acting possessed feeling and refinement; although her talents were confined to the narrow sphere of melodrama. When Macready became lessee of Drury Lane, Miss Huddart was engaged for principal characters in the legitimate drama, playing Lady Macbeth, Portia, Constance, Mrs. Beverley, Mrs. Haller, Mrs. Oakley, etc., with the eminent tragedian. Many original parts fell to her share, establishing the clever actress firmly in public favour. She joined Phelps in the management of Sadler's Wells, and for seventeen years continued to fill a leading position on the boards of that admirably conducted theatre. For a short period she directed the Marylebone Theatre. But her health unfortunately gave way, and she was compelled reluctantly to retire from the profession she loved so well. Domestic troubles supervened, and a painful disease prevented her working for her children and an improvident husband. Public sympathy, accompanied with substantial assistance, helped this gifted woman to bear her many afflictions. She did strive bravely to the end. Her Majesty the Queen not only subscribed to her fund, but daily sent a carriage which was placed at the invalid's disposal. Her medical advisers had suggested open-air exercise to the dying actress, which her own scanty means could not procure. She died at her residence in the New-road, a sad instance of the mutability of human affairs.

HENRY MARSTON (BORN 1804).

HENRY MARSTON made his appearance at Drury Lane Theatre, during W. J. Hammond's tenancy, as Benedick, in ' Much Ado about Nothing.'* The part of Beatrice was sustained by Mrs. Stirling, her first appearance at Drury and in that character. Henry Marston, a judicious actor, sustained his well-earned reputation for nearly half a century. He was one of our best representatives of Shakespearian characters —every sentence was given by him in scholarly style, and was exact without flourish or straining after new ideal readings

* October 31, 1839.

or startling effects, a practice too frequently
resorted to by modern aspirants for theatrical renown, heedless of their great master's
instruction on their art, conveyed by Hamlet
to the players.   Marston's circumstances not
being flourishing, added to a long illness,
induced Mr. Henry Irving to place his
theatre at Marston's disposal for a benefit,
May 29, 1879.   This yielded a sum of
£400, to comfort the old actor's remaining
days.

SAMUEL PHELPS, 1804—1878.

SAMUEL PHELPS, born 1804, commenced
his bread-winning as a printer at Baldwin's,
Blackfriars.   In the same office, picking up
type, worked Douglas Jerrold.   Phelps
always cherished a secret inkling for the
stage, and resolved to test his powers at
a small private theatre, then standing
in Rawstorne-street, Goswell-street.   Earl
Osmond, in Monk Lewis's ' Castle Spectre,'
was the ambitious printer's first essay.

Jerrold, at the request of Phelps, attended the performance to report progress. Next morning, when they met at work, Phelps, very anxious to hear his fellow-workman's opinion, tried many little stratagems to draw him out, but not a word escaped the lips of the future author of ' Mrs. Caudle's Lectures.' At last Phelps broke ground :

' Did you like me in Osmond ?'

Reply : ' No ; I did not. Stick to your printing ; you'll never earn twenty-five shillings a week by spouting.'

Phelps asked no other question that morning, but pursued his way—went on the stage, endured the usual rubs of fortune, until he found himself engaged to act leading tragedy at the Haymarket. Transplanted to the more genial soil (for legitimate acting) of Old Drury by Macready, a careful observer of merit, Phelps played much and many characters —sometimes great, sometimes small— from Father Joseph in 'Richelieu' to the

Jolly Captain in the 'Prisoner of War,' Macready's policy. One night our actor was a whale, the next a minnow. Phelps was allowed generally, when Macready retired from the stage, to be the first tragedian left to us. His management of Sadler's Wells Theatre for eighteen years was a highly creditable, if only partially successful endeavour to create a taste for legitimate plays and good acting in a region that hitherto delighted in outrageously improbable dramas of the worst school. Fancy a piece supposed to instruct styled 'Jack Ketch!' Phelps swept the Augean stable clean. Liberality and good taste now ruled, and Sadler's Wells became one of the most popular places of amusement in London. Phelps joined Falconer and Chatterton's company at Drury Lane. 'Manfred' was produced, and Phelps played Byron's misanthropic recluse; Macbeth, King John, Cardinal Wolsey, Shylock, Sir John Falstaff, Lord

Ogleby, Sir Peter Teazle, Sir Pertinax Macsycophant, Bailie Nicol Jarvie, Mr. Oakley, etc., all acted with ability and correct judgment, with no straining after new readings or false interpretation—fair, smooth personations of character—*not points*. Phelps lived to give contradiction to Jerrold's prophecy of twenty-five shillings a week receiving £80 and frequently £100 a-week for his performances. Samuel Phelps died November 6th, 1878, aged 74. His last appearance at Drury Lane was as Sir Peter Teazle for a benefit. His final appearance on the stage was at the Aquarium as Cardinal Wolsey, in 'Henry the Eighth.' His strength deserted him in this effort; he was led from the stage, never to return. A clever artist, and upright man in every sense—public and private— and an ornament to the theatrical calling.

MRS. WAYLETT (MISS COOKE), 1807—1855.

MRS. WAYLETT (Miss Cooke), born at

Bath in 1807, appeared on the Bath stage at seventeen ; her vivacity and charming appearance established Harriet Cooke as a favourite with her townsfolk.   She soon found a home in London.   Managers were all too glad to avail themselves of her talent. Her voice was very clear and beautiful, in ballad-singing perfection.   Her quick appreciation of comedy rendered her a worthy rival to Vestris.   No vocalist equalled Mrs. Waylett in her ballads, ' I'd be a Butterfly,' ' Kate   Kearney,'   ' My   own   Bluebell,' ' Come   where   the   aspen   quivers,'   etc., composed by Alexander Lee, and sang by Mrs. Waylett with a popularity previously unknown. She quitted Drury Lane through severe illness, never to return, dying after protracted suffering at the age of forty-eight.

JOHN BALDWIN BUCKSTONE, 1802—1879.

J. B. BUCKSTONE (one season at Drury with his own ' Mary Ann,' under Bunn's management). Little Buckey was born at Hoxton near London, in September, 1802, and was originally intended by his parents for the medical profession. This, like many other good intentions, was frustrated by young Buckstone's intense love of acting. He quitted the paternal roof, joined a strolling company, wandering from one village or town to another, and playing tragedy,, comedy, pantomime—everything in short that fell in his way. In later times folks would have stared to read in the Haymarket bills—Othello, or Iago, Mr. Buckstone ; but in his salad days he performed both these characters at Epsom. Chance gave him an opportunity of wooing the Comic Muse, and he more or less remained faithful to her ever after. It is many years since his merry unctuous voice first made the old Coburg ring with laughter at ' I want my goats ' (he played a goat-herd in a drama of his own concocting, called ' The Bear Hunters '). An immense favourite

on the Surrey side was little Buckey. At
the Adelphi he rose high in the estimation
of more refined judges, his numerous
dramas contributed largely to the popularity
of this favourite house. Though good in
legitimate comedy, he excelled most in
drollery and in roguish fun and humour.
As examples may be instanced his Sir
Toby Belch and his Launcelot Gobbo.
Buckstone's management of the Haymarket, extending over twenty-five years,
was in the main successful. Many of his
comedies still keep the stage. ' Married
Life,' ' Rural Felicity,' ' Single Life,' ' The
Rough Diamond,' and ' Good for Nothing '
(rendered so popular by Mrs. Fitzwilliam's
admirable acting), retain all their popularity.
' Green Bushes,' ever green from its constant revival, forms a standing dish for
Adelphi gourmands. ' Lord Dundreary,'
that really brilliant addition to the peerage,
first made his bow at the Haymarket with
Buckstone. His lordship drew immensely,

to the great benefit of manager and actor. On a certain occasion Buckey's rather numerous family wanted him to take them to see a pantomime at Drury Lane, as a good father ought to do. He wrote thus to me for a box :

' DEAR STIRLING,

'Will you ask Mr. Chatterton if I can have a large box for Saturday morning next, 6th February? my party being seven or eight: Mr. B., Mrs. B., Miss Annie B., Miss Lucy B.; Master J. B., Master R. N. B., Master Sidney B., and perhaps a little one in.

'Truly yours,
'J. B. BUCKSTONE.'

A change at length came over the fortunes of the Haymarket. Bad seasons, an increasing family, loans raised at exorbitant rates, reduced Buckstone's circumstances to a low ebb. A benefit at Drury Lane, well supported, proved merely 'a drop in the well.'   Ruin came with old age, and all its attendant ills—a sad reverse to one who had for so many years administered to the amusement and enjoyment of the public.   He died October 31, 1879.

W. H. PAYNE, 1804—1878.

W. H. PAYNE, 1804, PANTOMIMIST.—This clever man began his career studying under Grimaldi, Bologna, etc., at Old Sadler's Wells Theatre.   Payne played clown at the Pavilion, under Wyatt and Farrell's management, in 1826, and previously to that in a temporary theatre—the Old Whitechapel Workhouse.   By industry and continuous improvement, Payne found himself in Covent Garden Theatre, playing Giant in a Christmas pantomime.   Engaged by Farley on those boards for thirty-five years, with little intermission, our pantomimist continued to please ; always a student of his art,—gesture and action supplying speech.   Payne played at Drury

Lane a season or two with Bunn, St. George in 'St. George and the Dragon.' At an advanced age he continued to act in ballets of action and pantomime openings, with his clever sons, fresh and active as of yore. Old Time appeared for awhile to have forgotten him, so lightly did age seem to affect W. H. Payne. Serious pantomime expired with him. He shuffled off this mortal coil December, 1878, aged seventy-four.

DICKY FLEXMORE.

DICKY FLEXMORE, one of the Grimaldi school of clowns, alas! now extinct. A 'fellow of infinite jest' was Flexmore; agile, humorous and quick at invention. For many seasons he delighted the juvenile visitors to Old Drury's pantomimic displays. He was the life and soul of fun and frolic. Marrying the daughter of Auriol, the popular French clown, he spent his wedding-trip profitably, travelling with his father-in-law's troupe through the South of

France, combining profit with pleasure. Dicky represented his Satanic Majesty in a ballet dressed in the orthodox fashion—black, horns, tail, pitchfork. The 'circus' gave two shows each day—mornings and evenings. To save trouble, Dicky travelled in his downstairs attire, wrapped up in a cloak, on a caravan, Frequently passing through road-side villages, the wicked demon would jump down, rush into a cottage, seize anything that happened to be on the table, and jump into his caravan again, always choosing the peasants' dinner-hour. Shrieks, prayers, and lamentations filled the air, the affrighted peasants naturally supposing the actual Satan had paid them a visit; the mimic one meanwhile quietly drinking their wine and swallowing their viands in high glee. Flexmore died playing clown at Covent Garden.

DICKY USHER.

DICKY USHER, Drury Lane clown, in-

ventor of the Washing Tub and Geese on
the Thames ; first exhibited for his benefit,
1828. Dicky launched his fragile bark at
Waterloo Bridge stairs, for his Goose
voyage to Westminster. I need not say
his benefit proved how much the public
are governed by impulses. Dicky, in his
clown's dress, on a penny trumpet accompanied a dance of geese on the stage to a
popular tune ; the affrighted birds flapping
their wings and jumping like mad. ' How
was this accomplished ?' the reader may
perhaps inquire. Simply by placing sheets
of heated iron on the stage ; the geese, turned
out of their cage, screamed with pain, and
could not stand still. This cruel exhibition
brought down thunders of applause.
Luckily for Dicky, in those days, there
existed no Society for the Protection of
Animals. He drove a tandem with four
cats—always stolen on his arrival in each
town. These wretched animals, fixed by

collars to a pole ; if they faltered, a sharp spike behind propelled them forward. Their painful task accomplished, out the feline sufferers were driven with a whip. Dicky Usher was father-in-law to Mrs. Alfred Wigan (Miss Pincott). Her mother, Mrs. Pincott, married the clown.

HOWELL.

OLD HARLEQUINS *versus* PANTALOONS.— Howell, many years harlequin at Drury Lane, exchanged his magic bat for pantaloon's crutched stick. At a rehearsal of a pantomime, Stanfield, the eminent painter, came on the stage to give instructions relating to his scenery; and observing Howell tottering about, he thus addressed him :

'Mat, my boy, you've helped me to solve a problem. Till this moment I could not guess what was done with old harlequins; I see now, they're cut up for pantaloons. Ha, ha !'

MISS GRANT (LADY MOLESWORTH).

MISS GRANT, vocalist (Lady Molesworth), made her *début* at Drury Lane, Friday, 5th October, 1827, in the operatic drama ' Rob Roy.'

DIANA VERNON, *Miss Grant*, (her first appearance on any stage).

ROB ROY, *James Wallack.*

BAILIE NICOL JARVIE, *Mr. Liston.*

Her last appearance on the stage was as Hymen in ' As You Like It,' in Macready's revival of that play.

EDWARD ELTON.

EDWARD ELTON, 1828, appeared at the Garrick Theatre, Goodman's Fields ; from thence he removed to the Haymarket, playing leading characters, Macbeth, Shylock, etc. Macready secured his services for Drury Lane, where he played second parts to his manager. He was a judicious actor, and much esteemed. Elton was unfortunately drowned in the *Pegasus*, wrecked on its way from Edinburgh to London. All on board the ill-fated vessel were lost.

> ' Speaks not the hollow-sounding sea
>   Of what hath been, and no more shall be ;
>   Of days that are passed, of friendship gone,
>   Of hopes that shone, but to set in night ?'

Elton left a wife and family to bewail his sad loss, placed in a painful position, thus deprived of their support. The Guild of Literature and Art came humanely to their help and rescue. Dickens, Hood, Mark Lemon, Jerrold, Sir Edward Bulwer Lytton. manfully worked for the widow and children. A large sum was collected by benefits and subscription, placing the family beyond want.

LAURA HONEY.

LAURA HONEY, a delightful vocalist. and comedy actress, first appeared at the Strand in a piece of Leman Rede's ' Loves of the Angels.' Mrs. Waylett sang a telling ballad, directed to Mrs. Honey's eyes : 'Those eyes, those eyes, so beautiful and rare!' Yates engaged her for the Adelphi. Her progress speedily attracted the notice of Bunn and Charles Kemble. A ballad, 'O my beautiful Rhine,' with imitations of Tyrolese singers, attracted great attention. Endowed with rare musical gifts and a lovely face, Mrs. Honey had not long to woo fortune : it wooed her. She retired from the stage, and died at an early age (thirty-two), lamented by all who knew her kindly nature and real worth.

JOHN REEVE.

JOHN REEVE acted a season at Drury, and one at Covent Garden. The study and restraint necessarily practised to give perfection to legitimate comedy, ill agreed with Reeve's erratic mind; words he scarcely ever learnt perfectly, relying on his

grimace, ready wit, and unflagging humour.
He returned to his favourite quarters—the
Adelphi, and there reigned supreme, the
life and soul of Buckstone's dramas. Who
could forget his creation of Beadledom,
Gog Magog in the 'Wreck Ashore?' As
Billy Taylor, Bonassus, Young Norval,
Cupid, etc., he was without a rival ; these
creations of his fertile imagination remain
his own. His devotion to wine broke up a
strong constitution, and at last reduced his
universal popularity to mere toleration, a
sad falling off for poor John ; this he could
not endure. He quitted his loved Adelphi,
sickened, and, at an early age, died from
vexation and humbled pride. The stage
could well have afforded to lose a better
actor ;—it could not well lose a more worthy
man than John Reeve, kind, charitable,
humane to all that required help, whose
open purse, when it contained anything,
was always ready to aid the needy or to

serve a friend—a readiness not always reciprocated, as the following brief correspondence with Yates will show. John Reeve, being 'out at elbows,' wrote to Yates :

'DEAR FRED,

'I'm in a fix—£120 cash : help me.

'Brompton-row,

'Feb. 12, 1837.'

Reply from Yates:

'Adelphi, 13th inst.

'DEAR JACK,

'Ditto, for double your amount : help yourself.

'F. YATES.'

WILLIAM MURRAY.

WILLIAM MURRAY, proprietor of the Edinburgh Theatre, played in his youthful days at Drury Lane. This accomplished scholar and actor was lineally descended from Lord John Murray, secretary to

Prince Charles Edward in 1745. Murray's management of the old Theatre Royal, Edinburgh, was perfect. I sent him a copy of my adaptation of Dickens's " Christmas Carol." Murray wrote to me immediately after reading the piece.

' DEAR STIRLING,

　　' Just read the " Christmas Carol " to my company: we are all in tears; Tiny Tim made us cry, young and old. You have adapted the story admirably.

　　　　　　' Yours truly,

　　　　　　　　' WM. MURRAY.

' E. Stirling, T.R., Adelphi.'

CLARA FISHER.

CLARA FISHER, a remarkably precocious child actress—and one of the few that retained her talent in mature years ; pretty and engaging. This clever girl acted Albert in ' William Tell ' with Macready ; Prince

Arthur in ' King John ' to Edmund Kean's King John. Her solo performances exhibited much merit. When approaching womanhood she emigrated to America, where good acting is not so general ; her merits were quickly recognised, and the New World became her home and abiding-place. Many years she occupied a foremost place among the actresses of the United States.

MRS. FITZWILLIAM (FANNY COPELAND).

MRS. FITZWILLIAM (Fanny Copeland), a charming popular singer and actress—the original representative of many of Dibdin, Buckstone, and Poole's best characters, in their respective plays. ' Our Fanny,' as she was familiarly called by her theatrical brethren, lived for many years to delight her audiences by genuine acting, not *from* nature, but nature itself ; a melodious voice, united to an ever-smiling, good-humoured face, rendered Fanny Copeland a favourite on and off the stage. Among her many creations may be mentioned Nan in 'Good for Nothing,' Madge Wildfire, and Cicely Homespun in 'The Heir at Law.' The Hay-market, Lyceum, Olympic, Covent Garden, and Drury Lane, rang again and again from year to year with her joyous peals of laughter, re-echoed by her hearers, ever alive to true merit and natural acting. She died in 1858.

WILLIAM CRESWICK (BORN 1813).

WILLIAM CRESWICK originally made his *début* at a small theatre in the Commercial-road East, opened by an author employed to write for Astley's, one Amherst. "Master Collins" (Creswick) played the part of a poor murdered Italian organ-boy — one of the first victims to a new style of killing called 'burking' (from the first malefactor named Burke). Creswick worked hard for many

years in the country towns. He was fortunate enough to attract the attention of Miss
Mitford and of Thomas Noon Talfourd.
The talented authoress of 'Our Village'
selected him to act Cromwell in her tragedy
of 'Charles the First.' Ion he played quite
to the author's (Talfourd's) satisfaction. I
introduced him at the Lyceum (under Pen-
ley's brief management) in a piece of my
writing, 'Silver Crescent.' He afterwards
entered into a profitable partnership with
Mr. Shepherd at the Surrey Theatre, and
had constant London engagements. He
made an American trip in 1871, and
another in 1877-78 to Australia. Report
states that our colonial brethren like Creswick vastly.

MADAME CELESTE (BORN 1814).

MADAME CELESTE. At Tottenham-street
Theatre, in a pantomimic drama, 'The
French Spy,' came before the public the

clever Celeste (wife of an American, Mr. Elliott), of French birth and Spanish origin. This remarkable woman at an advanced age appears to have lost little of her youthful grace and vigour. Her performance of Miami in the ' Green Bushes ' continued to attract and delight till a period quite recent (1874). A dancer and actress of surpassing excellence. La Folie delighted all observers. Her acting at Drury Lane in serious pantomime became a feature. The first piece (' Prediction ') in which Celeste attempted to speak English, was acted at the Pavilion ; I played her lover. As joint manageress with Webster, she by her industry and taste contributed not a little to the popularity of the Adelphi.

JOHN RYDER (born 1814).

John Ryder, an actor of talent. Anything Ryder attempts is well performed ; frequently in leading characters, seconds, and what is theatrically termed 'heavy business ;'—grave senators, irate fathers, kings and tyrants. Ryder's elocution is very good. He puts it to a profitable purpose by teaching for the stage and the bar.

MRS. STIRLING (FANNY HEHL) born 1816.

Mrs. STIRLING (Fanny Hehl), born 1816 ; daughter of Captain Hehl, one of the military secretaries at the War Office. This gallant officer's extravagance brought his clever child on the stage. To earn her living became imperative. She commenced at the Coburg, with Davidge, in a very humble position, delivering messages at a small theatre in the East. Her next engagement, playing chambermaids in low comedy. Farrell saw and engaged her for the Pavilion Theatre, Whitechapel-road. Possessing personal attractions and talent, Farrell starred the young actress as 'Miss

Fanny Clifton,' for the nonce. She accepted the name of Stirling, marrying Edward Stirling, the writer of this book, and proceeded with him to Liverpool, Manchester, and Birmingham, becoming a favourite in all these towns. Her name quickly travelled to London. Bond, then manager of the Adelphi, made her an offer, which was accepted. She played Victorine, etc., establishing herself with the London public at once. She appeared at the Olympic and at Drury Lane, under Hammond's management. She came out as Beatrice, in 'Much Ado about Nothing,' at the Haymarket, with Webster. She sustained leading comedy parts, Constance, in the ' Love Chase ;' Sophia, in the ' Road to Ruin ;' Rachel, in the ' Rent Day ;' Peg Woffington, etc. Mrs. Stirling's style is essentially of the French school, elegant and piquant ; her skilful by-play fills up the scene with much effect. Her popularity at charitable meetings, held to assist her theatrical brotherhood, is unbounded. After-dinner speeches, touching wittily upon topics of the day, appeals to pockets, etc., form one of the attractions at these gatherings that could ill be spared. Her eloquent words produce sensible effects on her hearers' purses. This clever woman is the legitimate successor of Mrs. Jordan and Mrs. Glover, equally attractive in characters requiring deep feeling. Her Cordelia, Julia in the 'Hunchback,' Belvidera, etc., ranked high in dramatic art, winning universal popularity, justly deserved and well sustained.

SIMS REEVES.

SIMS REEVES, the eminent vocalist and first tenor of our time, made his *début* at Drury Lane during Jullien's management. Reeves had previously sung aud acted with Rouse at the 'Eagle' saloon (now the

Grecian), then conducted by Rouse, at a very small remuneration. By study and meritorious industry, Reeves gradually arrived at his now distinguished station. Endowed with a splendid voice, and having acquired a perfect knowledge of his art, he became a musician of the first class. Such attainments place this clever artist first among English singers. At the musical festivals held in our stately old cathedrals, Reeves is unapproachable. His melodious voice reverberates through those time-hallowed walls with grand effect and force. It is marvellously inspiring to his listeners, aiding the effect of the sacred music.

G. V. BROOKE.

GUSTAVUS VAUGHAN BROOKE, was born in Dublin, and received a good education at Trinity College. At thirteen he saw Macready play William Tell at the Theatre Royal. This event settled

Brooke's future career. The stage, nothing more or less, was his choice. He acted William Tell at fourteen in Dublin. This led to a tour through Ireland, Scotland, and England. Master Brooke became a 'juvenile' Roscius. Possessing a fine voice, a handsome figure and features, with great devotion to the stage, he rapidly made his way to place and distinction· Reports began to reach the London managers of the youth's talent. Macready bid first for the new actor, and he was duly engaged to act at Drury Lane. When he arrived in London, his first visit was directed to the theatre. Entering the green-room, he saw posted up a cast of the 'Merchant of Venice'—*Salarino*, Mr. G. V. Brooke, his first appearance; and a notice, that on Friday, 'Othello' would be acted—*Othello*, Mr. G. V. Brooke. In an instant the cast was torn down, and Salarino stalked out of the theatre, vowing vengeance. A few months after this escapade I offered him an opening at the Olympic. The following is the reply I received :

> 'Theatre Royal, Greenock,
>
> 'September 8th, 1843.

'MY DEAR SIR,

'Ever since the very disgraceful conduct of the Drury Lane Management towards me, I have almost buried myself in oblivion. With regard to visiting the metropolis under existing circumstances, it will be utterly impossible for some time ; and even then, I will candidly confess to you that nothing but a *most tempting* offer would induce me to leave the provinces. I am aware that a great number of persons think me little better than a madman for acting in the manner that I have done and am doing, but I am determined to see my way clearly and "bide my time." I open the Ayr Theatre for

the Caledonian Hunt on the 25th instant.
However, I shall drop you a *weekly hint*
of my locality, and shall feel happy to hear
from you and profit by your counsel and
advice, and in the meantime,

  'I remain, dear sir,

   'Yours very truly,

    'GUSTAVUS V. BROOKE.

 'P.S. I leave here on the 18th instant
for Ayr.'

He did accept an engagement after a
few seasons at the Olympic, appearing this
time in 'Othello' with marked approbation.
The daily press unanimously agreed upon
the talent and merits of the new tragedian.
Comparisons were made with the elder
Kean, Young, Macready and Charles
Kean. Even in these tests he came out
well: inferior to none, equal to all. Fortune smiled, wealth and position awaited
this highly-gifted man. Alas! he neg-

lected to accept the gifts of the fickle goddess, letting slip his chance for fame and fortune. After a voyage to America, a short season at the Marylebone Theatre, and a tour in the provinces, flattering offers came from Australia—he accepted them; made money in Melbourne and Sydney, only to lose it again in speculations—public gardens, mines, etc. He returned to England to replenish his purse—too late! his attraction had passed away. He married Miss Avonia Jones, a clever American artiste. Disappointed by his reception in the old country, he resolved to bid it adieu for ever, to return to Australia and make it his future home, hoping to restore his shattered circumstances. To will, was to do. He embarked in the ill-fated vessel the *London* for Melbourne, taking his only sister to live with him in the colonies. How futile are all human endeavours! After leaving port, a terrible storm arose in the Atlantic, scarcely four days from the coast of Ireland. The ship became a total wreck, sinking with all on board but a few sailors, that took to the only boat left. Brooke's courage, resignation and fortitude in this hour of death and mortal agony were beyond all praise. Day and night he worked at the pumps, inspiring by his example others to do their duty. His sister drowned in her cabin, bereft of every hope, he heroically kept his post. All lost—boats staved—roaring waves sweeping over the doomed ship. No living soul on board but Gustavus Brooke. Alone he stood leaning on the companion-door, waiting for eternity. The sailors in the boat urged him to leave the wreck: 'No, no; good-bye! remember me to my friends in Melbourne!' were his last words. The vessel lurched, sank, and with it one of the bravest of the brave. His idol

Shakespeare's words apply to this true man's fate :

> ' A brave vessel,
> Who had no doubt some noble creatures in her,
> Dash'd all to pieces.   O ! the cry did knock
> Against my very heart !   Poor souls ! they perish'd.
> All lost ! to prayers, to prayers ! all lost !'

DION BOUCICAULT (BORN 1822).

DION BOUCICAULT, actor and dramatist, was born in Dublin in 1822, his father being a French *émigré.*   His mother was a Miss d'Arcy, related to the wealthy family of the Guinnesses.   The famous Dr. Dionysius Lardner acted as guardian to Dion, who was educated at University College, London, and was originally intended for a civil engineer.   At twenty-two he had acquired sufficient knowledge of his profession to obtain diplomas from the Society of Engineers, but inspired with other thoughts and views, he would not wait for an appointment.   His predilections

were for the stage, and I it was who introduced him to it, forty-three years since.
He came to me at the Adelphi, requesting
that I would take the Princess's Theatre
(then building) for him. Modest this,
without any actual experience or much
capital, but great fertility of brain, and not
a trifling quantity of Irish assurance. I
did not take the theatre, nor did Dion
manage it. He more prudently joined
Mrs. Macready's company at Bristol—
played there originally Jack Sheppard.
In Irish characters he speedily made his
mark, and no one now excels Boucicault in
his personations of his own countrymen,
refined, natural, and genuinely humorous.
Stage traditions are not suffered to intrude
themselves into his conceptions of the
'Boys of Green Erin.' He began at an
early period of his theatrical career to write
for the stage, and continues to do so up to
the present time. As a playwright he is

as fresh and brilliant as ever. It is not to
be denied that he largely profits by foreign
dramatic literature, especially the French,
though much original work too has
emanated from his facile pen. His first
great success was at Covent Garden
Theatre in 1841, under Madame Vestris's
management. His five-act play entitled
' London Assurance' was most welcome to
the town and to all admirers of comedy,
and maintains its rank as one of the best of
modern days. It is always attractive and
always pleasing.

ORIGINAL CAST.

SIR HARCOURT COURTLY, *William Farren*
(the elder).
CHARLES COURTLY, *James Anderson.*
DAZZLE, *Charles Mathews.*
MARK MEDDLE, *Harley.*
MAT HARKAWAY, *F. Mathews.*
DOLLY SPANKER, *Keeley.*

COOL, *Meadows.*
SIMPSON, *W. H. Payne.*
LADY GAY SPANKER, *Mrs. Nesbitt.*
GRACE HARKAWAY, *Madame Vestris.*
PERT, *Mrs. Keeley.*

Dion's pen had from this date full employment. Managers eagerly bid for his productions, which generally proved profitable. Charles Kean at the Princess's constantly availed himself of this skilful penman's ideas—'Faust and Marguerite,' 'Louis the Eleventh,' 'Corsican Brothers,' 'Ann Blake,' 'Vampire,' etc. In the last-named piece he acted to some purpose, wooing and winning the heart and hand of pretty Miss Agnes Robertson, known as 'the pocket Venus.' A voyage to the United States brought increased reputation and grist to the mill. On his return to England, he produced at the Adelphi his farfamed Irish drama, 'The Colleen Bawn,' previously acted in New York. This pathetic drama, freely adapted from an Irish tale, 'The Collegians,' by Gerald Griffin, created a *furore*. Houses crowded nightly for many months to enjoy really good acting. Mrs. Boucicault played the part of the poor ill-used Colleen, and Dion Myles-na-Coppaleen. Nothing could exceed the pathos and comic humour that he invested this part with. A series of pieces followed, of which the most famous was 'The Octoroon.' A difference between Messrs. Webster and Boucicault brought the latter to Drury Lane in 1862, supported by his wife, Madame Celeste, Atkins, Ryder, and others. Here the Irish maiden 'Colleen' kept her ground, until the 'Relief of Lucknow' came, in all its horrors and Oriental pageantry : well-acted—soldiers, pipers, guns, drums, cannon and mutineers, false Rajahs, devoted women, gallant men, comic Irishmen, stupid Englishmen, etc., filled up the measure of India's rights and wrongs. Astley's was the next scene in Boucicault's speculative efforts—a Circus converted into a really elegant theatre. 'Lucknow' was relieved now on the Surrey side of the Thames. Boucicault made a mistake with his pantomime, trying to restore the old style—that of gesture for speaking. This failed, and failed signally. 'The Trial of Effie Deans,' an adaptation of Scott's 'Heart of Mid Lothian,' did well. His Counsel for the Prisoner was perfect, and might have passed muster in a real Court of Law. A romantic odd impossibility filled his brain—that of converting a dirty stable-yard and equestrian stabling into a fashionable theatre, surrounded by beautiful gardens. This magical alteration was to be accomplished by a Joint Stock Company—the usual bank for impossibilities. The following is a copy of the Prospectus he issued :

'NEW THEATRE COMPANY, LIMITED.

'Capital, £125,000 [modest], in 5000 shares, of £25 each, with power to increase. Deposit on application, £1 per share; and on allotment, £2 per share. It is anticipated that not more than £12 will be required to be called up. Two months' interval between each call.

'*Patrons :* The Duke of Wellington; the Duke of Leinster; the Marquis of Donegal; the Marquis of Normanby; Earl Grosvenor; the Earl of Malmesbury; the Earl of Hardwicke; the Earl of Sefton; the Earl of Dudley; Sir John Shelley, M.P.; etc., etc.

'*Directors :* H. C. Cobbold, Esq., New Bridge-street, Blackfriars; J. W. Cusack, Esq., 12, Lancaster-gate; E. Edwards, Esq., Adelphi Chambers; Lieutenant-Colonel Napier Sturt, M.P., Portman-square; Gerard de Witte, Esq., The Greenways, Leamington.

' *Bankers :* Ransom and Co., Pall Mall.

' *Auditors :* Quilter, Ball, and Co.

' *Broker :* J. B. Richards, Austin Friars.

' Offices, 9, Cornhill.

· ' *Secretary :* H. J. Montague [the popular actor].

The conditions and anticipated profits of this speculation were carefully considered and calculated. Dividends at ten per cent. during the building of the theatre, might reasonably be expected when the theatre opened. Mr. Boucicault's services to manage the enterprise were secured for one-third of the net profits. Although a large number of shares were privately subscribed for, the ignorant public held aloof, slow to believe or accept this very promising undertaking. Fancy twenty per cent. and a life privilege of walking in a beautiful garden theatre, ornamented by grottos, cascades, and endless attractions (on paper)! The whole thing fell flat : city men did not believe in it ; West-enders simply laughed at this flight of Dion's fancy. The idea of converting into a paradise a slough of despond, in one of the worst of neighbourhoods, surrounded by shabby, tumble-down, ramshackle houses, inhabited by the poorest class of petty tradesmen and waterside labourers! Presto! by the wand or silvery tongue of Wizard Boucicault, all these difficulties were to vanish, giving place to a reality out-rivalling the Hesperides of old! Many leading men of rank came to see this temple of Dion's muse; dukes and lords 'a-many.' Among the distinguished visitors was the Earl of Carlisle, Viceroy of Ireland. An Irish servant (Farrell) received his lordship in his master's absence. Paddy quickly claimed acquaintance with Carlisle, hoped his Excellency was well, and his sister Lady Elizabeth—'long life to her. Och, she was a rael beauty.'

' What were you, then ?'

FARRELL : ' I carried coals up to her ladyship's room at the Castle, my lord—bedad, I'd 'ave carried the Castle if she'd asked me.'

This effusion had its effect—a crown-piece and a good laugh at Hibernian impudence.   Lord Carlisle wrote to Boucicault on this matter :

' March 15, 1863.

' DEAR SIR,

' I think the Irishman showed a very proper zeal to bring his two sovereigns together.

' Your faithful servant,

' CARLISLE.'

After the non-success of Astley's, and after incurring heavy losses, Mr. and Mrs. Boucicault sought another field for their exertions.   The Amphitheatre, Liverpool, received them ; and a piece was localised for the purpose. This expedient had been tried in several towns in America. Originally a French piece, in the clever hands of Dion it became his own, and under the title of 'The Streets of Liverpool—a Sensation drama' (a word coined by Boucicault to express wonder, astonishment, grief, joy, or any other thing to catch the people) proved a gold mine. Easily altered, it did duty in almost every town in Great Britain, and finally found a resting-place at the Princess's Theatre, as 'The Streets of *London;*' drawing for Vining (lessee) and the author, £16,000.

> 'Royal Hotel, Glasgow,
>
> 'March 13.

'DEAR STIRLING,

'"When the wind blows, then the mill goes;" and Fortune's gale is making my mill spin round like blazes. I have developed a new vein in the theatrical mine, and one in which you can have an interest beyond that you always feel in my success.

'I have tried the bold step of producing, originally in the provinces—a sensation drama, without aid or assistance of any kind.   The experiment has succeeded.

'I introduced 'The Poor of Liverpool' —a bobtail piece—with local scenery, and Mr. Cowper in the principal part.   I share after £30 a night, and I am making £100 a week on the * * * * * thing.

'I localise it for each town, and hit the public between the eyes; so they see nothing but fire.*   *Et voilà.*

'I can spin out these rough-and-tumble dramas as a hen lays eggs.   It's a degrading occupation, but more money has been made out of guano than out of poetry.

' Believe me, very sincerely yours,

'DION BOUCICAULT.'

* One of the scenes was a burning house.

Boucicault's retirement from the stage in his native city (Dublin) brought himself and his talented wife back again to London. Second thoughts Dion knew to be best. They did not retire, luckily, but produced ‘Arrah-na-Pogue,’ a first-rate Irish drama, in which Shaun the post, in Boucicault's hands, became the leading feature. Drury Lane accepted a realistic serio-drama, entitled ‘Formosa,’ of rather questionable plot; introducing certain ladies of the *demi-monde* in their home circles. The attempt, hazardous as it was, proved monetarily a hit. Chatterton and the author cleared more than £12,000 between them; Shakespeare, in the same house, being played to empty benches; such is the taste of our time. Another trip to America succeeded, from which Dion returned to Old Drury with a cargo of fun and extravagant effects wrapped up most ingeniously in the ‘Shaughraun.’

This clever Hibernian drama yielded a rich harvest. Moya, well looked and acted by Mrs. Boucicault; Conn O'Kelly, the ' Shaughraun ' (Vagabond), performed by Boucicault himself, was the soul of whim, humour, and roguish expedients. His associate, Tatters, a dog, talked of but not seen, helped his master right well through the piece. In 1872, with the aid of Planché, he wrote, concocted, and put on the stage at Covent Garden, a spectacular piece, fantastical, musical, and certainly novel, called

' BABIL AND BIJOU ;
or,
THE LOST REGALIA.'

There were a large number of dancers, actors and actresses, singers, Amazonian warriors ; together with a perfect dramatic aquarium of oysters, crabs, cockles, seals, periwinkles, sea-lions, sea-horses, sharks, alligators, sword-fish, devil-fish, lobsters, etc.,—a silver city, a real coral grove, a river of life, and mountains in the moon. Here was a dainty dish for the most imaginative to feed upon ; yet the undiscerning public refused to honour the repast with their presence. It signally failed. Boucicault sailed to America, leaving his 'mountains of the moon' to take care of themselves, conveying orders through the Atlantic cable. This costly experiment of trying how much money may be lavished on production of novelty quickly squandered a fortune to no purpose whatever, save paying a host of persons a salary for six months.

In 1876, Boucicault returned once more to the United States, and New York for a time became his chosen residence. He is ever at work. New pieces constantly appear in the American bills from his facile and indefatigable pen. Our Lope de Vega of the present day, the brain and industry of this prolific dramatist approach infinity. Adieu, Dion Boucicault ! in the words of your native land, ' Cead-mille-failthe,' when you come to Old England again.

He did return, April, 1880, playing once more his favourite Conn, at the Adelphi.

MISS GLYN (MRS. DALLAS).

MISS GLYN (Mrs. Dallas) made a very favourable *début* at the Olympic Theatre, under Spicer's management, in ' Lady Macbeth,' Wednesday, January 26th, 1848. Possessing a fine person, and a melodious voice, with the advantages of Charles Kemble's instruction, she could scarcely fail. Her Cleopatra won favour with critics and public alike. Antony might well lose the world for such a woman. For the three following years she acted at Sadler's Wells, with the late Mr. Phelps. She greatly improved before her appearance at Drury Lane, 1854, in a play of Fitzball's, with Barry Sullivan. Her performance of the Duchess of Malfi was much admired. Miss Glyn of late years has devoted her abilities mainly to public readings and professional teaching.

BARRY SULLIVAN (BORN 1824).

SULLIVAN commenced his theatrical career with Seymour, in Ireland, as a vocalist, singing in ' Love in a Village.'
YOUNG MEADOWS, *Mr. Barry.*
ROSETTA, *Miss Smith* (niece to the Dowager
Countess of Essex, Miss Stephens).

Sullivan tried Scotland next. Under the judicious tutelage of William Murray he rapidly advanced in his art. Copeland engaged the young actor for his leading tragedian at the Amphitheatre, Liverpool. Here he made a lasting impression. Webster, ever desirous of novelty, intro- duced the Liverpool favourite to a London audience at the Haymarket. Sullivan's

Hamlet, Romeo, and Evelyn in ' Money,' received the highest praise. Golden harvests in the provinces followed this London success. A trip to Australia added largely both to fame and profit. On his return he entered into an engagement at Drury Lane with E. T. Smith, and afterwards with Chatterton. In his management (though well carried out) of the Holborn Theatre, Sullivan did not realise money. Strictly legitimate · plays carefully put on the stage did not draw. He made a fresh tour of the provincial towns, with renewed popularity and emolument. His earnings average £7,000 per annum. This large amount produced by one man's talent is extraordinary, and refutes the cry that the legitimate drama is in its decadence. This excellent tragic actor received an offer of £10,000 for twelve months' performance in America. This he accepted: reappearing as Richard

the Third, at Drury Lane, after its fulfil-
ment, on September 23rd, 1876.   Sullivan
is unquestionably one of the best tragedians we now have : ever careful and un-
ceasingly industrious.

BARRY SULLIVAN AND THE TROMBONE
PLAYER.—Sullivan, acting in the Potteries,
requested the leader of a small orchestra
to let him have the wind instruments
behind the scenes in the fifth act of
' Richard the Third.'

'Sir, I c-a-n-t' (*with a stutter*).

OFFENDED TRAGEDIAN : 'Sir, I insist ;
send up your wind.'

AGITATED FIDDLER : 'I—I—I——'

ENRAGED ACTOR : 'Where's the manager?'

The manager answered for himself.

'Here, sir.'

'Mr. Elphinstone, your conductor objects
to let me have his wind instruments on the
stage for the march in the fifth act.'

'Poor fellow ! he stutters and is deaf.'

BARRY : 'Why did he not tell me so ?'

IRATE VIOLIN : 'Yes ; and I—I—I'll tell you more, sir : there's only one wind, a trombone. Am I to—to—to cut him in two, send up one half to you, and keep the other half in the orchestra ?'

This silenced Richard ; he proceeded to Bosworth Field minus wind.

MRS. HERMAN VEZIN.

MRS. HERMAN VEZIN, an actress of high and rare merit, played the leading business at Drury Lane several seasons, under Mr. Chatterton's direction. Her rendering of Shakespearian heroines displayed a keen perception of the great poet's creations. Gentle Desdemona or queenly Constance lost no effect by Mrs. Vezin's acting. She re-appeared at Drury Lane, September, 1876, as Queen Elizabeth in Cibber's version of ' Richard the Third;' and in 1878 as Paulina, in a revival of 'The Winter's Tale.

CAROLINE HEATH (MRS. WILSON BARRETT).

MISS HEATH was engaged at Drury Lane to act Margaret in the 'King O'Scots' (*Fortunes of Nigel*). Originally she acted at the Royalty with a company of amateurs. Her grace and promise of ability attracted the notice of the late Charles Kean, then manager of the Princess's Theatre, and he engaged her. Year by year her improvement was so marked, that Mrs. Charles Kean gave up many of her leading characters to the young actress. This brought reputation, and placed Miss Heath in a foremost position. Several times her Majesty commanded her attendance at Osborne and Windsor, to read Shakespearian plays to the Royal Family. On a journey to Balmoral, the Queen happened to catch sight of Miss Heath standing on the platform amidst a crowd of ladies at Perth. Her Majesty immediately recognised her, talking and walking up and down until the train was ready, when, graciously accepting a bouquet from her and shaking her hand, she kindly bade her farewell. This condescension of the Queen naturally caused the fair actress to be 'the observed of all observers.' Miss Heath, or rather Mrs. Barrett (for such is her married name), continues to act and please, chiefly in our large provincial towns. She appeared at the Princess's Theatre, the scene of her early triumphs, 1877-8, in Mr. W. G. Wills's new play of 'Jane Shore.' The play was universally popular, and its success, though reflecting great credit on the author, must be mainly ascribed to Miss Heath's admirable impersonation of the unfortunate heroine.

MRS. HOWARD PAUL (MISS FEATHERSTONE) 1833—1879.

MRS. HOWARD PAUL (Miss Featherstone) appeared first at the Strand in 1852, and made a most favourable impression. Her fine *contralto* voice, her handsome features, her graceful deportment, added to considerable ability, rapidly placed her in a foremost position. She played and sang in 'The Beggar's Opera,' as Captain Macheath, for many nights. Smith engaged her for Drury Lane. Lord Glengall wrote a piece to introduce her to a Drury Lane audience, 'Cook and Housekeeper.' Her entertainments given with her clever husband, Howard Paul, proved very lucrative. 'Patchwork,' written and compiled by Howard, filled their purses. She died in June, 1879, lamented by all who knew her.

AMY SEDGWICK (BORN 1835).

MISS AMY SEDGWICK commenced her theatrical career at the Royalty Theatre in 1853, as an amateur, under the assumed name of 'Miss Mortimer.' Her first engagement of consequence was at Manchester, under the management of Knowles. She rapidlly improved, gradually leading the business. Transplanted to the Haymarket, her talents at once established Miss Sedgwick as a popular favourite. In October, 1866, she played Lady Macbeth at Drury Lane during the engagement there of Mr. Phelps and Mr. Sullivan. If not a great performance, it was fairly rendered, and with care and effect. Honoured by her Majesty's patronage, and married to a gentleman of the medical profession, this clever and amiable lady has now retired into private life.

ADAH ISAACS MENKEN, 1864.

ADAH MENKEN (female Mazeppa 1864) treated originally with the managers of Drury Lane to appear; but E. T. Smith bade higher for her appearance at Astley's. I first suggested Menken's engagement to Smith, telling him of her success in

Vienna.   He replied in this somewhat laconic fashion :

' DEAR STIRLING,

     ' Thanks. Menken may go to Drury Lane or the devil; she won't do for me. She was kicked out of America.

                              ' E. T. SMITH.'

Smith altered his mind ; she did perform at Astley's, and to some purpose, clearing for her own share £200 a week for four months.   Adah Menken was something more than an equestrian heroine.   She was a woman of culture and refined habits.   A French Creole by birth, a life of varied trials and strange adventure had not extinguished her love for poetry or her habits of refinement.   A volume of poems written by Menken, and dedicated by his permission to Charles Dickens, is sufficient to corroborate this assertion.   Alexandre Dumas,

John Oxenford, Dickens, etc. were among
her many distinguished friends and admirers. She died at an early age in Paris;
her perilous ride ending in a quiet corner of
Père La Chaise.

'Theatre Royal, Astley's.
' Monday,

' DEAR MR. STIRLING,

' Your note came when I was out,
so pardon my not replying sooner. I had
hoped to see you lately, that I might explain my reasons for deferring the finale of
our farce. There are unavoidable reasons,
that is, just at present. If I may have the
pleasure of seeing you, I can show you why
I am compelled to delay.

' Believe me, dear Mr. Stirling,
' Yours truly,
'A. I. MENKEN.'

HENRY IRVING.

HENRY IRVING.—Thisdistinguishedactor

dates originally from Manchester. Irving worked in small provincial companies with a determined will and steadfast purpose to rise in the art he had chosen. His first appearance in London was in 1859 at the Princess's Theatre (manager, Augustus Harris, sen.), in a romantic drama, entitled 'Ivy Hall,' written by the late John Oxenford. Irving's character was a very small one. He rapidly made his merit felt. Boucicault engaged him to play a leading part in a new piece, ' Hunted Down,' produced by Miss Herbert at the St. James's Theatre. Fortune's tide now set in. Managers sought the rising artist. Fortunately for him the late Mr. Bateman, lessee of the Lyceum, saw his merit and secured his services for his opening, to act with one of his daughters. This venture did not, however, hit the public taste. ' The Pickwick Club ' gave Irving an opportunity of displaying his capability for eccentric comedy. His

Jingle would have satisfied Dickens ; to the life the clever scamp walked and talked. Jeremy Diddler in ' Raising the Wind ' followed, a part of the same pleasant type ; more serious matters succeeded. Bateman, a keen observer, saw something original in Irving's acting, hitherto unrecognised. This he cultivated. Mathias in ' The Bells ' took the play-going world by surprise—a fine conception of a painful subject. It raised Irving highly in estimation. Then followed a series of plays. ' Charles the First :' Irving's Charles was a really historical portrait of the most unfortunate of the Stuart kings. In ' Eugene Aram,' the actor's peculiarities of form, voice, and expression told in his favour. The remarkable criminal lived again in all the horrors of repentant remorse and mental suffering. Richelieu, after Macready's perfect personation of the great French statesman, appeared a hazardous venture, albeit Irving succeeded. This performance paved the way for Hamlet, carefully put on the stage. Irving made his bow as the Prince of Denmark under very favourable circumstances, prepared for him by Bateman. The result, it is needless to say, was a most unprecedented run of Shakespeare's play, numbering over two hundred nights. Old and young stagers agreed that it was a masterly performance. 'Macbeth' was the next trial. In this a lack of physical strength operated against the actor's intentions greatly ; it never reached the point 'Hamlet' achieved. In 'Othello' again Irving lacked force in the terrible impassioned scenes of jealousy and revenge. Cleverly conceived, it never reached within many degrees Denmark's misanthropical prince ; nor did immediate comparison with Salvini act favourably for Irving's Othello. The Italian's fine acting of this part undoubtedly left Irving in the shade, despite our English artiste's acknowledged great merits—and they are many. Philip of Spain, in Tennyson's 'Queen Mary,' afforded an excellent opportunity for the exercise of Irving's careful study. He gave us a complete portrait of Mary's bigoted, unloving husband : dress, deportment, manner, a living resemblance. Irving's rule—' No pains, no gains.' Louis XI. added new laurels to his fame. This wily, tyrannic, royal hypocrite was played to perfection by the talented artiste. Not a phase of the despicable monarch's character was left unrevealed. He lived, talked, and thought, resuscitated by Irving's consummate skill, aided by Philip de Commines' masterly historical chronicle of the tyrant's life and death. Mr. Irving assumed the sole management of the Lyceum on Boxing-night, December 26, 1878, re-appearing in 'Hamlet,' his first and greatest Shake-spearian personation. The part of

Ophelia was allotted to Miss Ellen Terry; crowded audiences nightly attested to Irving's popularity. After a season of unprecedented success, a holiday trip to the Mediterranean, as the guest of Baroness Burdett-Coutts, brought his labours in 1879 to a prosperous termination: £36,000 taken during his short season.

1880, 'Merchant of Venice.' Shylock, H. Irving; Portia, Ellen Terry. Shylock in Irving's hands became a veritable success. The clever graceful acting of his fair Portia added much towards the 'Merchant of Venice's' extraordinary run. Irving never acted better; the relentless Jew was a Rembrandt-like portrait of life and action.

HENRY J. MONTAGUE, 1863.

This brilliant young actor commenced his theatrical career at Astley's Theatre, in 1863, under Boucicault's management.

He applied to me for an engagement. I introduced him to Boucicault, and he was engaged to play 'utility': his first step, Counsel for the Defence in 'Effie Deans'—a part Dion had made his own. Boucicault being obliged to leave for Brighton, I gave it to Montague, and he did it well. This was followed by 'Nicholas Nickleby,' and a secretaryship in the New Theatre Company. Montague rapidly rose in his profession—young, handsome, endowed with a constant flow of vivacity and an ardent love for the stage, resolving to rise, he did. At the Prince of Wales's Theatre he found himself in a genial atmosphere of comedy. Luck or fortune allotted him important and suitable parts, that brought out his qualifications for gentlemanly humour. Encouraged by this success, he entered into co-partnership with James and Thorne, and opened the

Vaudeville. As Jack Wyatt in the ' Two Roses '—their opening piece—he made a great impression. Always ambitious, he resigned his partnership, and quitted the Vaudeville for the sole management of the Globe Theatre. Here he produced some of the best comedy-dramas of the day : ' Partners for Life,' ' Forgiven,' ' False Shame,' and notably, ' Cyril's Success.' He joined Boucicault in a trip to America in 1872. In New York he became a favourite after his first performance. Public favour increased nightly ; step by step he won their feelings and hearts, especially those of the ladies. Endowed with a manly, sympathetic nature, ever ready to assist the necessitous, Montague was always doing kindly acts in his quiet way. This clever favourite actor died suddenly at San Francisco, California, August 12th, 1878. Montague had taken a company there to play ' Diplomacy.' The sad event, so unexpected, greatly affected the playgoing public of San Francisco. A mother and two sisters remain to mourn a dutiful son and a loving brother. Thus departed Henry J. Mann ('Montague') at the early age of thirty-five, in the prime of manhood and in the plenitude of his talents.

MONTA GAINSBOROUGH.

MISS GAINSBOROUGH, a young actress of considerable talent, was engaged by Mr. Chatterton (1876) to play Lady Rowena in 'Ivanhoe,' at Drury Lane. In the higher walk of the drama, Juliet, Pauline, etc., Miss Gainsborough displayed much intelligence, graceful deportment, and good delivery.

ELLEN WALLIS.

MISS WALLIS made her appearance at Drury Lane, 1875, as Cleopatra in

' Antony and Cleopatra.' The new actress possesses considerable ability for her vocation, a musical voice and a graceful deportment, aided by youth and assiduity. Her rendering of Shakespeare's wily Egyptian Queen was well conceived. It would have required a more subtle soldier than ' Antony ' to have resisted such endearments. Miss Wallis played the popular characters of Juliet and Pauline charmingly. Her first appearance on the public stage was at the Queen's Theatre, as Mildred Vaughan in a drama of the late Mr. Watts Phillips —' Amos Clark.' This personation at once established her claims to public acceptance. In the provincial towns she is an especial favourite, drawing good houses and winning golden opinions from all classes. She reappeared at Drury Lane in September, 1878, as Hermione in the ' Winter's Tale.'

ACTRESSES ENNOBLED BY MATRIMONIAL ALLIANCES.

Miss Fenton (the original ' Polly ' in the ' Beggar's Opera '), DUCHESS OF BOLTON.

—*Miss O'Neill*, LADY BECHER.

Mrs Nesbit, LADY BOOTHBY.

Harriet Mellon, DUCHESS OF ST. ALBANS, —won two matrimonial prizes : first, a rich banker, Mr. Coutts ; secondly, a poor Duke, the Duke of St. Albans, who gladly accepted a banker's widow with £70,000 a year.

Fanny Braham (daughter of Braham the singer), FRANCES, COUNTESS OF WAL-DEGRAVE.

Miss Foote, COUNTESS OF HARRINGTON.

Miss Stephens, COUNTESS OF ESSEX.

Miss Paton, LADY LENNOX.

Miss Fortescue, LADY GARDINER.

Miss Grant, LADY MOLESWORTH.

Mrs. Canning.—An Irish actress originally. Her son, GEORGE CANNING, became Prime Minister. He never neglected writing to his mother daily, whatever the pressure of business might be on his time.

Miss Farren, COUNTESS OF DERBY* (grandmother of the present Earl). 'The Oaks' were established by her husband, the Earl, for her. A ballad opera, written by General Burgoyne, called 'Fair Maid of the Oaks,' commemorated the event.

* 'Miss Farren of Drury Lane (Countess of Derby), at the Preston Jubilee Guild, August 3rd, 1802, dressed in the top of fashion. About six o'clock, the Earl and Countess of Derby (the beautiful young actress) entered their house in Preston, from Knowsley, to dinner. They were in a coach and six; Mrs. Farren came with her daughter. We are sorry to say the distress for beds has obliged some to submit to exorbitant prices. One family gave fifty guineas for three beds in a very obscure part of the town.'— *Preston Chronicle*, 1802.

Miss Brunton, COUNTESS OF CRAVEN.

*Maria Tree,** THE HON. MRS. BRADSHAW.

Mdlle. Mercandotte, COUNTESS OF FIFE.

Miss George, LADY MACDONALD STEPHEN-SON.

Miss Lewis, MRS. GENERAL BOARDMAN.

Miss Bolton, LADY THURLOW.

Miss Helen Faucit, LADY MARTIN.

While endeavouring to chronicle this

* Miss M. Tree, was an excellent actress and singer. She was the original Clara in 'The Maid of Milan' —a clever drama by Howard Payne—in which she introduced the song that obtained a world-wide renown, 'Home, sweet home.' Mary Copp in 'Charles the Second'—another capital piece from Howard Payne's pen—afforded Miss M. Tree an opportunity of displaying a vein of humour in a humble station, perfectly opposed to all the parts she had hitherto sustained. The cast of this excellent two-act comedy was as follows :

KING CHARLES THE SECOND, *Mr. Charles Kemble.*
EARL OF ROCHESTER, *Mr. Jones.*
EDWARD (*a page*), *Mr. Duresel.*
CAPTAIN COFFIN, *Mr. Fawcett.*
LADY CLARA, *Mrs. Faucit.*
MARY, *Miss M. Tree.*

brief history of our National Theatre, Drury Lane, I have carefully avoided alluding to the personalities of private life connected with the actors and actresses that have from time to time trod these almost classic boards. Silence has all the prudence and none of the vices either of simulation or dissimulation. Let us think and speak with Burns on this theme :

> ' Then gently scan your brother man,
>   Still gentlier sister woman ;
>   Though they may gang a kennin' wrang,
>   To step aside is human.'

BOOK IV.

DRAMATIC ANA AND THEATRICAL VARIETIES, WITH
AN ACCOUNT OF CURIOUS OLD PLAYS, ETC.

PLAYBILLS FIRST PRINTED, OCTOBER, 1587.

JOHN CHARLEWOOD 'had lycensed to him
by the whole consent of the assistants, the
onlye ymprinting of all manner of billes for
Players, provided that, if any trouble arise
hereby, Charlewood to bear the charge.'
An entry on the Books, Stationers' Hall.

Bill Posting, 1587.—'They used to set
up their billes upon Postes, some certain
days before, to admonish the people to
make resort to their Theatres.'

PETITION AGAINST A THEATRE, 1596.

The inhabitants of Blackfriars petitioned
the Lords of the Council against a common
playhouse, about to be built in Blackfriars,
fearing the evil effects and immorality of

such a building, and inconveniences brought on themselves.

EDWARD ALLEYN, FOUNDER OF DULWICH COLLEGE.

1614.—Alleyn was a player, and proprietor of the 'Fortune' playhouse in Golden-lane. To this he added the Keepership of the Royal Bear Garden. Old Aubrey relates that the devil appeared while he was acting one on the stage. This so frightened him that he quitted the stage and acting for ever. He endowed his College in 1617, and became its first master. He also gave £800 per annum (a large sum at that time) for the maintenance of one master and one warden (who must be unmarried), and always bear the name of ' Alleyn,' or Allen; four fellows, three of whom must be clergymen, the fourth an organist ; besides six poor men and six women, with twelve boys, who are all to be educated till the age of fourteen or sixteen, when they are to be apprenticed to some trade. The building is called 'The College of God's Gift.' Alleyn died in 1626, and was buried in the College Chapel.

Edward Alleyn, founder of Dulwich College, Ben Jonson, and Shakespeare—a triumvirate of talent—frequently spent their evenings together at a tavern called the Globe, near Blackfriars Theatre. George Peele, the dramatist, a member of the club, wrote a letter to one Marle, his friend :

'I must desyre that my syster hyr watch and the cookerie booke you promised may be sent bye the mann, I never longed for thy company more than last nighte—We were all verye merrye at the Globe, where Ned Alleyn did not scruple to affirme pleasantly to thy friend "Will," that he had stolen the speeches about the qualityes of an actors excelencye in "Hamlet" from conversations manyfold which had passed between them, and opinions given by Alleyn touching the subject. Shakespeare did not take this tale in good sorte ; but Jonson put an end to the strife by wisely remarking, " This needs no contention, Ned, you stole no doubt," do not marvel, have you not seen him acte times out of number ?

' believe me yours sincerely

'G PEELE.'

BURBAGE AND KEMP.

The author of ' The Return from Parnassus,' says that 'he is not accounted a gentleman that knows not Dick Burbage and Will Kemp. There's not a country wench that can dance ' Sellinger's Round,' but can talk of Dick Burbage and Will Kemp.' Burbage was the original Richard the Third. Kemp was inimitable in the part of clown.

BURBAGE'S EPITAPH.

Burbage, Shakespeare's friend, and the

original representative of his great tragic characters. For perspicuity, wit, and brevity, his epitaph stands alone : ' Exit Burbage.'

SHAKESPEARE'S WILL.

He forgot his wife entirely, making his will. A line was inserted giving her his second-best brown bed and hangings, witnessed by Burbage and Condell.

SHAKESPEARE AND BEN JONSON.

PUNNING.—SHAKESPEARE, BEN JONSON. —Shakespeare, so the story runs, being very friendly with Jonson, stood godfather to one of Ben's children. Asking his brother dramatist in a pleasant way what gift he ought to bestow?

' Whatever you please, Will.'

' I've been thinking,' said the bard, ' I'll give the boy a dozen Latten spoons, and thou, Ben, shalt translate them ;'—in allusion to Jonson's knowledge of the Latin tongue. —*Harleian MS.*

SUPPOSED ORIGIN OF SHAKESPEARE'S 'MERCHANT OF VENICE.'

A note in Warton's 'Observations on Spenser's Faerie Queene,' informs us that Shakespeare drew his fable from an old ballad, nowhere to be met with but in the Ashmolean Museum, where it was deposited by that famous antiquary, Anthony à Wood: 'A song shewing the crueltie of Gunatus, a Jew, who, lending to a merchant an hundred crowns, would have a pound of his flesh because he could not pay him at the time appointed.' A story of the same nature is related in the Life of Pope Sixtus V.,—a wager between Paul Sicchi, a merchant, and a usurer, Samson Ceneda, a Jew. A report of the transaction was brought to the Pope; he sent for the parties, saying, 'Contracts should be fulfilled when made,' bidding Sicchi cut a pound of flesh from any part of the Jew's body; advising him to be careful, ' for if you cut but a scruple more or less than your due, you shall certainly be hanged.'

PAYMENT OF DRAMATIC AUTHORS IN SHAKESPEARE'S TIME.

The following statement is contained in a book of Notes and Memoranda, made by Henslowe, a manager of playhouses. (This curious record is in the archives of Dulwich College.) Henslowe's price for a new play never exceeded from eight to sixteen pounds ; but shortly after, the price rose to twenty and twenty-five pounds ; and the second day's performance added to the author's profits. A prologue fetched from five to twenty shillings. Shareholders of theatres derived great gains from performances. In 1602, ten pounds were paid to ' Burbidge's players ' for acting ' Othello ' before Queen Elizabeth.

WILLIAM PRYNNE, 1633.

Committed to the Tower for offending

Charles I. and his court ; sentenced to lose his ears and stand in the pillory ; to have a book of his writing, entitled 'Women Actors, Notorious and Infamous,' burnt publicly before his face. It happened that about six weeks after the publication of this diatribe the Queen acted a part in a pastoral comedy at Somerset House. Archbishop Laud, next day after the Queen had acted her pastoral, showed Prynne's book against plays to the King, informing him that it had been purposely written against the Queen and her acting, whereas it was published six weeks before the pastoral comedy was acted. 'A lie has short legs:' Laud speedily learnt the truth of this trite proverb ; imprisonment and the scaffold followed in succession rapidly.

CURIOUS CUSTOMS CONNECTED WITH THE PATENT OF DRURY LANE.

'Her Majesty's servants attached to the theatre, if passing through Windsor in the exercise of their calling, may partake of a dinner at the Castle. The lessee of Drury Lane is entitled to wear the Royal uniform, and to shoot over the Windsor estates.' This grant was made to Killigrew, the first patentee, by Charles II., and has never been repealed.

BRASS CHECKS.

Checks used at Drury Lane, in the reigns of Charles II. and James II., were of brass, with the amount of admission on one side, and the King's head on the other. They are very scarce now.

FIRST INTRODUCTION OF HORSES ON THE STAGE AT DRURY LANE.

' 1669, July the 11th.—To the King's Playhouse, to see an old play acted of Shirley's, called ' Hyde Park,' the first acted with horses. A moderate play; an excellent epilogue spoken by Beck Marshall, the first female actress that appeared on the stage.'—*Pepys.*

MOVEABLE SCENERY was first introduced by Sir William Davenant, lessee of Drury Lane in the reign of Charles II.

At the end of the performance a clown or jester recited a rambling string of verses, termed a 'jig,' the actors all knelt on the stage and prayed for the King or Queen.

KILLIGREW, THE FIRST LESSEE OF DRURY LANE, went with Charles II. to Chatham Dockyard, to view a ship on the stocks. The King asked Killigrew if he did not think he should make an excellent shipwright? The wit replied that he thought his Majesty would have done better at *any* trade than his own.

DUKE'S AND KING'S COMPANIONS.

In January, 1672, the playhouse in Drury Lane took fire, and was demolished, with sixty houses. The managers of Drury Lane and Covent Garden united (Duke's and King's Companies), resolved to open but one theatre. This was in 1682. The speculation did not prove profitable for directors or actors. The play commenced at four o'clock. Ladies of fashion used to take the evening air in Hyde Park after the play.

WILLIAM WYCHERLEY.

William Wycherley, poet and playwright of Drury Lane, 1640, was highly patronised by the notorious Duchess of Cleveland. Being at Tunbridge Wells, he chanced to enter a bookseller's shop in the Well Walk, with a friend, just as the Countess of Drogheda, a rich young widow, happened to be inquiring for the ' Plain Dealer,' one of Wycherley's comedies.

' Madam,' said Mr. Faulkner (Wycherley's companion), ' since you are for the " Plain Dealer," here is for you' (*pushing Wycherley towards her*).

' Yes,' observed the dramatist, ' this lady can bear *plain dealing*, for she appears to be so accomplished that what would be compliment said to others, spoken to her would be *plain dealing.*'

'No, truly, sir,' said the countess, 'I am not without my failings, more than the rest of my sex; and yet, notwithstanding, I love *plain dealing,* and am never more fond of it than when it tells me of them.'

'Then, madam,' said Faulkner, 'you and the *plain dealer* seem designed by Heaven for each other.'

Wycherley speedily married her, without the consent of the King (Charles II.). This brought the poet into disgrace. The Countess was jealous of him to distraction, and could never endure him out of her sight. They lived in Bow-street, Covent Garden, over against the Cock Tavern. When he dined there with friends he was obliged to leave the windows open, in order that his lady might see there were no women in the company.

GEORGE FARQUHAR.

George Farquhar, born at Londonderry 1678 ; of good birth and family, chose the actor's profession from love of it. He quitted the stage owing to a sad accident. Using a sword instead of a foil in Dryden's ' Indian Emperor,' he unfortunately killed a brother performer, Vasquerly, 1698. He produced a comedy at Drury Lane, ' Love and a Bottle,' 1700. He furnished another comedy to Drury, ' A Constant Couple.' The ' Inconstant ' followed, and afterwards ' The Recruiting Officer,' ' Sir Harry Wildair,' ' Stage Coach,' ' Twin Rivals.' His last and best-known comedy was the ' Beaux Stratagem.' During the rehearsals he was taken ill, and died before its production His friend, Wilks, the comedian, found among his papers this expressive note addressed to himself :

' Dear Bob,

' I have not anything to leave thee to perpetuate my memory but two helpless girls ; look upon them sometimes, and think of him who was to the last moment of his life, thine,

'G. Farquhar.'

Wilks, to his honour, did look after Farquhar's daughters. He at once set to work procuring benefits for his friend's family.

ACTORS VAGRANTS.

Actors were vagrants in law, 1700. Wanderers, among which are common players of interludes, minstrels, jugglers, fencers, bear-wards, all persons pretending to be gypsies or wandering in the habits of such, pretending skill in palmistry, or the like, or to tell fortunes, and such as use any subtle craft, unlawful games or plays, begging, or running away from their wives, they were committed to the House of Correction, and there set to labour for three months. Think of this law, brethren of the sock and buskin—ye who have had the good-fortune to be born in a milder and more tolerant age.

HANDEL AND SIGNORA CUZZONI.

The lady objected to sing. Handel always maintained absolute rule over the singers and the band.

'You will not sing, madame, eh ?'

'No,' replied Cuzzoni.

'You are a devil, madame, but I will make you know that I am Beelzebub, the chief of the devils ;' and seizing her by the waist he swore that he would fling her out of the window. She never objected to sing again.

Handel, blessed with an enormous appetite, usually indulged it without stint. On one occasion he ordered a dinner for four at the ' Bedford,' Covent Garden.   Punctually to the hour fixed came Handel, asking where the dinner was ?

WAITER : ' Quite ready, sir, but the company are not arrived.'

' Da company, bosh ! I'm da company. I always eat for four.   Serve it directly.'

SALARIES OF ACTORS, AND PRICES OF ADMISSION TO DRURY LANE IN 1733.

Colley Cibber, from the time that he sold his share in the management till he quitted the stage, £12 12s. per week.   Theophilus Cibber and his wife received £5 each a week ; Mills junr., £3 ; Mills senr., £1 per day, and a benefit free of charge ; Johnson, £5 ; Miller, £5, besides a present of ten guineas ; Griffin, £4 and a present ; Shepard, £3 ; Hallam and his father (though the latter is of no service), £3 ; Mrs. Heron, £5 (raised from forty shillings last winter, yet refused to play several parts assigned her) ; Mrs. Butler, £3 per week.

The prices at the theatre were—4*s.* the boxes; 2*s.* 6*d.* the pit; 1*s.* 6*d.* first gallery, and 1*s.* the second, except upon the first run of a new play or pantomime, when the boxes were 5*s.*; pit, 3*s.*; first gallery, 2*s.*

VANBRUGH'S PROVOKED HUSBAND.

The ' Provoked Husband ': a comedy by Sir John Vanbrugh and Mr. Cibber.

CAST AT DRURY LANE IN 1770.

MEN.

LORD TOWNLEY (of a regular life), *Mr. Smith.*

MR. MANLY (admirer of Lady Grace), *Mr. Wilson.*

SIR FRANCIS WRONGHEAD (a country gentleman), *Mr. Bensley.*

SQUIRE RICHARD (son of Sir Francis, a mere whelp), *Mr. Parsons.*

JOHN MOODY (servant to Sir Francis, an honest man), *Mr. Suett.*

COUNT BASSET (a gamester), *Mr. Dodd.*

WOMEN.

LADY TOWNLEY (immoderate in her pursuit of pleasure), *Mrs. Brooks.*

LADY GRACE (sister to Lord Townley, of exemplary virtue), *Mrs. Ward.*

LADY WRONGHEAD (wife to Sir Francis, inclined to be a fine lady), *Mrs. Hopkins.*

MISS JENNY (daughter to Sir Francis, pert and forward), *Mrs. Forster.*

MRS. MOTHERLY (one that lets lodgings), *Mrs. Love.*

MYRTILLA (her niece, seduced by the Count), *Miss Heaph.*

MRS. TRUSTY (Lady Townley's woman), *Miss Barnes.*

Scene laid in Lord Townley's house, and sometimes in Sir Francis's lodgings.

A GOOD CAST.

ADDISON'S ' CATO.'

PORTIUS, by King George III. (then Prince George of Wales); MARCIA, by the

Duchess of Brunswick (Princess Augusta). Quin, the actor, was manager, and instructed the performers. Prince George spoke a prologue written by Mallet.

> CATO, *Master Nugent.*
> PORTIUS, *Prince George.*
> JUBA, *Prince Edward.*
> SEMPRONIUS, *Master Evelyn.*
> LUCIUS, *Master Montague.*
> SYPHAX, *Lord North.*
> DECIUS, *Lord Millington.*
> MARCUS, *Master Madden.*
> MARCIA, *Princess Augusta.*
> LUCIA, *Princess Elizabeth.*

This play was acted at Leicester House, Leicester Fields, now Leicester Square.

THEATRE, AMSTERDAM—CURIOUS CUSTOM.

'The actors are all of them tradesmen, who after their day's work is over, earn about another guilder a-night by perform ing kings and generals. The hero of the tragedy was a journeyman tailor, and his first minister of state a coffee man. The empress keeps an ale-house in the suburbs of Amsterdam.   When the tragedy was over, they played a short farce, in which the cobbler did his part to a miracle ; but he had really been working at his own trade, and representing on the stage what he acted every day in his own shop.   The profits of the theatre maintain a hospital, for as they do not think the profession of an actor here the only trade a man ought to exercise, so they will not allow anybody to grow rich in a calling that in their opinion so little conduces to the good of the commonwealth.'— *Tatler.*

LOVE IN A VILLAGE.

Drury Lane,
Monday, October 25th, 1770.
His Majesty's Company,
At the Theatre Royal, Drury Lane.

This day will be performed

' LOVE IN A VILLAGE.'

HAWTHORN, *Mr. Vernon.*

JUSTICE WOODCOCK, *Mr. Parsons.*

HODGE, *Mr. Davis.*

SIR WILLIAM MEADOWS, *Mr. Aicken.*

YOUNG MEADOWS, *Mr. Webster.*

LUCINDA, *Miss Colett.*

MADGE, *Mrs. Wrighton.*

DEBORAH, *Mrs. Bradshaw.*

ROSETTA, *Mrs. Baddeley.*

To which will be added :

' THE ELOPEMENT.'

HARLEQUIN, *Mr. Wright.*

CLOWN, *Mr. Grimaldi.*

PANTALOON, *Mr. Bunn.*

LOVER, *Mr. Benton.*

DRUNKEN VALET, *Mr. Chaplin.*

SCARAMOUCH, *Mr. R. Palmer.*

COUNTRY GIRLS, *Miss Simson, Miss Kirby.*

COLUMBINE, *Miss Colett.*

Places for the Boxes to be had of Mr. Fosbrook, at the Stage-door.

The Doors will be opened at half-past Five ; to begin at half-past Six.

Vivant Rex et Regina.

FIRST ORATORIO AT DRURY LANE, 1775.

The following is a copy of the play-bill of the first Oratorio at Drury Lane:

At the

THEATRE ROYAL IN DRURY LANE.

On Friday next, March 3rd, 1775,
Will be performed

' JUDAS MACCABÆUS,' an Oratorio.

First Violin and a Concerto, by Mr. BARTHOLOMEW.

And a Concert on the Organ, by Mr. STANLEY.

Tickets to be had, and places for the Boxes to be taken, of Mr. Johnson, at the

Stage-door of the Theatre, at a Half-Guinea each.

Doors to be opened at Five o'clock; to begin exactly at half-past Six.

Vivant Rex et Regina.

Pit, 5s.; First Gallery, 3s. 6d.; Second Gallery, 2s.

PENKETHMAN'S BOOTH.

MAY FAIR, 1776 (suppressed). Penkethman's celebrated booth, prematurely brought to a close in the West, was hastily removed to Greenwich. His company announced to open with a 'Mythological, Musical Ballet of Action.' Sad mishaps befel the gods and goddesses. Venus and Cupid travelled on foot from London; Mars got drunk in the town, on his arrival, and broke his landlord's head; Juno quarrelled with her husband Jupiter, and flew back to town in a return post-chaise; Mars was set in the stocks for the assault. But the worst

part, the most melancholy of all, was that
Diana, star of the company, ran off with a
jolly young waterman, who rowed the
chaste goddess from the Tower stairs in his
wherry.   It would seem that these disasters
retarded Penkethman's opening for a time ;
but, nothing daunted, he announced that he
had another Diana and a 'patient Grissel'
coming down by the next tide from
Billingsgate.

'PLAY UP, NOSEY.'

This vulgar saying was directed to a
poor Italian violin-player, Cervetto, in
Drury Lane orchestra.   His nose was unfortunately very large, on this account the
galleries always made fun of him ; at last
it became so bad that Cervetto was obliged
to quit the theatre.   A poet of the day
wrote thus :

> 'Have ye not roar'd from pit to upper rows?
> And all the jest was what ?—a fiddler's nose !
> Pursue your mirth, each night the joke is stronger,
> For as you fret the man his nose grows longer.'

In one of the most tender scenes in
'Lear,' Garrick relates how the house
silent, enraptured by the great actor's
genius, the long-nosed musician gave a
loud yawn ; this set all the people laughing.
The enraged manager sent for Cervetto
and demanded why he behaved so ? In
broken English poor Nosey apologised :
'Sare, I begs ten tausend pardons, sare ;
but *ven mooch* interested I always open *ma
mouths* and yawn very louds.' This excuse
did not satisfy 'little David ;' he was
forbidden to be so 'mooch' interested
again.

MACKLIN AT BARRY'S FUNERAL.

MACKLIN, attending the funeral of Barry
in Westminster Abbey, pressed forward
to look at the grave. A verger remon·
strated, telling him not to crowd.

'Tush !' said Macklin, ' I want to see an
exact representation of the ceremony, for I

don't know how soon I may be called upon to play a principal character in the same tragedy.'

ANECDOTE OF G. A. STEVENS.

G. A. Stevens (comedian, Drury Lane), actor and lecturer. Playing in a country theatre Lorenzo, in the ' Merchant of Venice,' Stevens, being very imperfect in the text, was hissed by the audience. Turning to Jessica, he addressed the people ·

' Oh, Jessica in such a night as this we came to town,
  And since that night have touch'd but half-a-crown ;
  Let you and I, then, bid these folks good-night,
  Lest we by longer stay are starvèd quite.'

MANNERS OF LADIES VISITING DRURY LANE, 1780.

' It could well be wished that ladies would be pleased to confine themselves to whispering in their *tête-à-tête* conferences at the opera or the playhouse, which would be a proper deference to the rest of the audience. In France, we are told, it is common for the *parterre* to join with the performers in any favourite air; but we seem to have carried the custom still further, as the company in our boxes, without concerning themselves in the least with the play, are louder than the players. The wit and humour of a Vanbrugh or a Congreve is frequently interrupted by a brilliant dialogue between two persons of fashion; or a love-scene in the side-boxes has been more attended to than that on the stage. I have seen our ladies titter at the most distressing scenes in " Romeo and Juliet," grin over the anguish of a Monimia or Belvidera, and fairly laugh King Lear off the stage. The whole behaviour of our ladies is in direct contradiction to good manners. They laugh when they should cry, are loud when they should be silent, and are silent when their conversation is desirable.'—*Connoisseur.*

STROLLERS, 1790.

'Our company are far above the usual paltry strollers who run about the country. These ladies and gentlemen are from the Theatre Royal, Drury Lane: they have been employed there, in the business of the drama, in a degree above scene-shifters and message deliverers— "My lord, the carriage waits;" "Lady Betty Modish." And the heroine of this company, who had been employed at Drury Lane as a dresser, now blubbers out Andromache or Belvidera ; the attendants on a monarch now strut as monarchs themselves ; mutes find their voices ; these message-bearers rise into heroes. The humour of our best comedian consists of shrugs and grimaces, he jokes in a wry mouth, and repartees in a grin ; in fact, he practises all those distortions that gained him applause in town, from the galleries, when he played as a super in pantomime. I was vastly pleased at seeing a fellow in the character of Sir Harry Wildair, whose chief action was a continual pressing together of the thumb and finger. I discovered Sir Harry was no less a person than Mr. Cliphit, the candle-snuffer at Old Drury. How strangely the parts in " Cato " were cast! Marcia was such an old woman, that when Juba came on with his " Hail, charming maid !" he could not help laughing. The after-piece was " Lethe," and the part of a Frenchman was played by a Welshman, who, as he could not pronounce a word of the French language, supplied its place by speaking his native Welsh.

' The decorations (in theatrical parlance, " properties ") of our company are as extraordinary as the performers. Othello raves about a checked handkerchief; the Ghost of Hamlet stalks about in a postillion's leathern jacket for armour; Cupid enters with a fiddle-case for a quiver. The apothecary of the town is free of the theatre for lending his pestle and mortar for a bell in "Venice Preserved." Macbeth dashes a pewter-pot at Banquo (glass would be expensive). Two of the mimic heroes wished to play " Richard the Third ;" when the curtain drew up they both rushed on the stage at once, shouting " Now are our brows bound with victorious wreaths." Amidst roars of laughter, they both went through the whole speech without stopping.'

AN IRISH PLAY-BILL.

KILKENNY THEATRE ROYAL.

By his Majesty's Company of Comedians.
    Positively the last night, because the Company go to-morrow to Waterford.

On Saturday, May 14, 1793,

Will be performed, by desire and command

of several respectable people in this learned Matrapolish,

For the benefit of Mr. Kearnes,
the Manager,

'THE TRAGEDY OF HAMLET, PRINCE OF DENMARK,'

Originally written and composed by the celebrated Dan Hayes, of Limerick, and insarted in Shakspeare's works.

HAMLET, by *Mr. Kearnes* (being his first appearance in that character), and who between the acts will perform several solos on the patent bagpipes, which play two tunes at the same time.

OPHELIA, by *Miss Prior*, who will introduce several favourite airs in character, particularly 'The Lass of Richmond Hill,' and 'We'll all be unhappy together,' from the Rev. Mr. Dibdin's Oddities.

The parts of the King and Queen, by directions of the Rev. Father O'Callagan, will be omitted, as too immoral for any stage.

Polonius, the comical politician, by a young gentleman, being his first appearance in public.

The Ghost, the Grave-digger, and Laertes, by Mr. Sampson, the great London Drury Lane comedian.

The characters to be dressed in Roman shapes.

To which will be added an Interlude, in which will be introduced several sleight-of-hand tricks, by the celebrated surveyor, Hunt.

The whole to conclude with the farce of

'MAHOMET THE IMPOSTOR.'

Mahomet by Mr. Kearnes.

Tickets to be had at the 'Goat's Beard,' in Castle-street, of Mr. Kearnes.

The value of the tickets, as usual, will be taken out, if required, in candles, bacon, soap, butter, cheese, potatoes, etc., as Mr.

Kearnes wishes in every particular to ac
commodate the public.

N.B.—No smoking allowed, or swearing.
No person whatsoever will be admitted into
the boxes without shoes or stockings.

A ROYAL DECREE.

The Elector Duke of Wurtemberg
issued the following edict in 1802 :

' His most Serene Highness, having with
great displeasure perceived that many
persons dare hiss during the public performances at the theatre, it is his Highness's will that in future any offender of
this description shall be taken out of the
playhouse by the military, and delivered
into the hands of justice for punishment.
His most Serene Highness further expects
that during his presence at the theatre,
no one shall hiss or applaud unless his
Highness himself, by his example, shall
give the signal for doing so.'

Not bad for a petty German potentate with a territory not so large as Yorkshire. Here was paternal government with a vengeance!

AN EDICT ADDRESSED TO THE PREFECT OF LYONS BY NAPOLEON I.

'French Theatres, Decree, 1802.— Government wishes the theatre to be at once useful and moral, and an entertaining establishment. You are therefore to refrain from bringing forward such pieces as are only remarkable for their obscenity, or the indecent wit they contain; such in which the wretched authors wish to substitute libertinism for dramatic genius. Select as much as possible the ancient and modern productions which are played at the French Theatre, and in the Theatre Louvois. Hold in high contempt all the rhapsodies of the inferior theatres of the capital. With respect to the opera and ballets, you are to reject all such as in any manner can wound delicacy and good manners.'

A decree of this character might with great propriety be issued in this present year of grace for the edification of the playgoers of Great Britain.

CURIOUS ANNOUNCEMENT.

Drury Lane Theatre, January 2nd, 1796. 'Recruiting Officer,' and 'The Children in the Wood.' A domestic misfortune having happened to the principal performer in the new pantomime, the public are respectfully informed that its representation must be postponed for a few days.

TOM SPRING.

Tom Spring, the polite box office-keeper of Drury Lane under Elliston's *régime*, was a worshipper of rank and title, and carried out the art of adulation to perfection. Precise, formal, a scrupulous dresser (*à la mode*), he received his customers at the Box-office with much mock grace and absurd servility. To a commoner booking places, he vouchsafed a bow and ' Thank you '; to a baronet, a radiant smile, two bows, and ' I am greatly obliged, sir ; ' to a lord, Spring bowed three times lowly, and ' felt honoured by his lordship's patronage '; marquises and dukes received bows without number; ' Graces ' and 'most noble,' with ' grateful thanks ' in profusion ; but if a Royal personage happened to appear, poor little Beau Spring's head almost touched the ground, while, with downcast eyes and reverential manner, ' Your Royal Highness ' was constantly repeated until his illustrious visitor was out of sight.

Courtly box-keeper ! your bland smiles and hollow servility would pass unnoticed in these matter-of-fact days. Bowing went out with Old Vauxhall Gardens, powdered wigs, pug-dogs, and pigtails.

ABSENCE OF MIND.

Harry Webb, comedian of Drury Lane, lessee of the Queen's Theatre, Dublin, produced 'Macbeth' with new scenic effects. Among the rest, clouds descended to conceal the exit of the Three Witches in the first scene. Webb, anxious to ascertain the result, passed from the stage to the front of the theatre, and peeping through an opening at the back of the boxes, saw but two witches instead of three 'meeting 'in thunder, lightning, and in rain.'

'Where's the other witch?' cried Webb, rushing behind the scenes, asking the prompter; 'fine him, sir—fine him a week's salary.'

' Please sir, it's yourself that missed the scene.'

' Bless me, so it was! Dear me, give

me a cloak, I'll go on in the next scene ; and fine yourself, Jenkins, five shillings for suffering me to neglect my business.'

' Sir ?'

' Yes, five shillings ; it ought to be ten shillings.   I'll take five.'

QUEER ADVERTISEMENT.

Queer advertisement, 1809, inserted in the papers, when Drury Lane was rebuilding : ' Drury Lane opens at the Opera House, Haymarket,the 10th of next month.'

'HAMLET' AT THE OLD ROYALTY THEATRE, 1818.

Carles, a good, legitimate actor, migrated from Drury to the East.   The old man generally during his performances had a little refreshment.   This was sent at eight o'clock each evening from a tavern opposite the stage-door.   A new pot-boy was sent with the pint of ale, crust, and cheese, and told by the landlady to give it to Mr. Carles. This he carried out to the letter. The stage was level with the street, and there was no one to direct him. 'Pots' hearing Carles's voice, hurried on the stage before the audience, just at these words in Hamlet's soliloquy, 'To be, or not to be.'

POTS: 'To be, to be sure, sir; here I be, pint o' ale and crust.'

He did not remain there long. A kick from the Royal Dane sent ale, crust, and the unfortunate bearer into Wells-street. No more Shakespeare that night. Whenever the Prince of Denmark entered, a titter accompanied him.

THEATRICAL JOCKEYSHIP.

Theatrical Jockeyship. — Race-course, Drury Lane; gentlemen jockeys, Elliston and Ducrow; equestrian stakes, £50 per week; won in a canter by Ducrow. Elliston, in order to give additional effect to a spectacle produced at Drury Lane on an Easter Monday, 'The Cataract of the Ganges,' engaged Ducrow's horses. One had to ascend a roaring cataract of real water, carrying a lady. The piece was rehearsed daily; the horses and their riders were in attendance, but no Ducrow. This went on for a week or two, till Manager Elliston grew uneasy. The horses by themselves were useless; no one could manage them. · He wrote to Ducrow, requesting his presence. The great man came.

ELLISTON : 'My dear Ducrow, where have you been? Your horses and men are in a fog. They cannot move without your direction. My piece will be ruined.'

DUCROW (*smiling*) : 'Sorry for that, but I cannot help it.'

'Not help it, man? What do you mean? You are engaged to appear here, sir·—here, Monday week.'

' No, no, governor ; you're wrong. My horses are ; not Andrew Ducrow.'

It was a fact; his name had been omitted in the agreement, only Ducrow's horses and riders named. Poor Elliston saw his position, and, with a sigh, gave the wily equestrian £50 per week more for Andrew Ducrow's services. All went well, and the piece proved a hit ; but Elliston paid the stakes to the clever jockey Ducrow with a very ill grace, be sure !

ANNOUNCEMENT. DRURY LANE PLAY-BILL.

Monday, November 22, 1819.

The public is respectfully informed that the Pit is filled to overcrowding fifteen minutes after the doors are opened— opened precisely at half-past six.

' RICHARD THE THIRD.'

GLOSTER, *Mr. Kean.*
RICHMOND, *Mr. Elliston.*

A SPEAKING PANTOMIME, BY GARRICK.

A speaking pantomime, written by Garrick, played at the Theatre Royal, Drury Lane.

April 10th, 1820.

'HARLEQUIN SHAKESPEARE;
or,
THE INVASION.'

Characters by Madame Vestris, Miss Povey, Mrs. Harlowe; Messrs. Munden, Harley, Keeley, G. Smith, Oxberry, Knight, and Gattie.

CAST OF 'OTHELLO' AT DRURY LANE, 1827.

OTHELLO, *Mr. Kean.*
IAGO, *Mr. Charles Young.*
CASSIO, *Mr. James Wallack.*
BRABANTIO, *Mr. Archer.*
RODERIGO, *Mr. Browne.*
MONTANO, *Mr. Mercer.*
DESDEMONA, *Miss Foote.*
EMILIA, *Mrs. Glover.*

SHAKESPEARE'S HOUSE, 1828.

A butcher's shop. When I saw it there was a board over the doorway, informing the public that ' This is Shakespeare's house : he was born here. A Horse and Cart to let.'

FALL OF THE BRUNSWICK THEATRE, FEBRUARY 20TH, 1828.

This dreadful catastrophe occurred to a theatre built on the ruins of the Old Royalty Theatre, burnt down. Mr. Carruthers, a city merchant, bought and opened the Brunswick. First, alas ! and only piece, ' Mermaid's Well ;' founded on Sir Walter Scott's romance. EDGAR OF RAVENSWOOD, *Mr. Osbaldiston.* The new building fell in during a rehearsal, killing many performers, and causing great consternation in London at the time.

MILTON STREET PLAY-HOUSE, 1828.

Formerly the 'Grub-street,' of poor poets. A chapel converted into a small theatre, by John Philip Chapman (proprietor of the

Sunday Times paper, and its originator). Chapman married Anne Tree, a sister of Mrs. Charles Kean, and thus became theatrical. His speculation paid, for he displayed tact and spirit in his management. He formed a capital company, including Ellen Tree, Mrs. Selby, Mrs. Egerton, Selby, G. Bennett, and Keeley. A star of the first magnitude, Edmund Kean, appeared at this queer little place. The Irish tale of 'The Colleen Bawn,' taken from ' The Collegians,' and dramatised by Boucicault in after years, was produced here. This first version, ' Eily O'Connor,' appeared in 1828. Chapman unfortunately was compelled to give up this theatre. Mercantile difficulties fell heavily upon a clever, generous man. Charles Kean, greatly to his honour, came to the rescue, assisting his sister-in-law and children. Milton-street Theatre resumed its original uses, and again became a sectarian chapel.

DROPPING H'S AT DRURY LANE

'Woodman's Hut,' a piece patronised by our grandfathers, crammed full of sensation, prominently a burning forest. A new actor was cast as one of three robbers, prime agents in villany and crime, Wallack and J. Smith being his fellow-scamps. Scene, a forest—the 'Woodman's Hut;' Time, Night. Three thieves enter to extremely cautious music (a rule in the old melodramas when anything wicked had to be done).

First Robber (the new comer to his comrades) : ''Ush ! I see a *nouse*' (pointing to the hut).

Second Robber (enjoying the joke) : ' No, Blunderby, it's a *nut.*'

Third Robber (Wallack) : ' No, fool, it's a *nabitation.*'

Roars of laughter greeted this wholesale dropping of h's. This was in 1831, under Elliston's management.

LITTLE PHIL STONE.

A Drury Lane character off the stage, a very small Majesty's servant, styled 'stage-property man'—very important to the well-doing of performances. Juliet could not commit suicide without the aid of this humble official; he supplies the poison. What would Macbeth do without daggers? Duncan would sleep on unharmed; Virginius' knife was quite as important as himself. Stone ruled his properties in a right royal fashion, selecting what he pleased, giving what he thought proper. A juvenile author of a farce objected to a sofa in one of his scenes. This roused Phil's ire (Phil, I must mention, lisped, and had little or no acquaintance with Lindley Murray).

'Not likes it, sir (*with a lisp*)?' 'That 'ere sofy not good enough for a farce? why, Mrs. Jordan and Mrs. Siddons 'as sot on it many a time. It'll last longer than your piece, I'll lay.'

Stone embarked his savings in a small tripe and sheep's-head shop, in a court near . Drury Lane—where he sold savoury relishes, hot sheep's-heads and baked potatoes. A good trade sprang up among the performers for Phil's snacks. One of the rogues told the little man that Macready had ordered a ' head and taters,' after his 'William Tell' one night. Here was honour! the great tragedian supping off one of his heads! Stone's wife prepared everything in apple-pie order— clean white napkin, cover, etc., Phil being ordered to carry the head upstairs to Macready's dressing-room. After the play comes a gentle tap at the sacred door.

Voice Inside : ' Who's there ?'

Reply Outside (faintly) : ' Sheep's-head, please, sir.'

Loud roar inside, and a rush to the door (tragic) :

'What the devil is that, sir?'

STONE: 'A hot 'un, Mr. Macready, sir, and browned *taters* for you—my wife seed to 'em herself.'

Down went the head, potatoes, and property-man; with threats and imprecations directed to heads in general—especially baked!

VAN AMBURGH, 'THE LION KING,' AT DRURY LANE.

This speculation of introducing wild animals and their tamer was Bunn's; it proved profitable, such was the people's taste! Empty benches to Shakespeare—full houses for caged lions, tigers, and leopards. Our Queen frequently honoured Van Amburgh's daring performances by her presence before and behind the curtain.

NAPOLEON III. AT A JUDGE AND JURY CLUB.

Garrick's Head, Bow-street, a club, founded and presided over by Baron Nicholson.   A burlesque court of law, famed for audacity, wit, and gross immorality, attracted high and low to its pestilential purlieux, Prince Louis Napoleon, then in exile, among the rest. He was entrapped by card-sharpers to play deeply, and of course lost. He gave bills to the amount of £600. These bills were negotiated by E. T. Smith, lessee of Drury Lane. Fortunately the prince discovered the fraud. ' Paulton and Co.' found themselves at the bar of the Old Bailey ; sentenced to two years' imprisonment, and Louis Napoleon's bills cancelled. Smith had not passed them, luckily for him. When Napoleon became Emperor, Smith had the impudence to write to him, asking permission to open a Cremorne Gardens in Paris ; but no reply was vouchsafed by the new occupant of the Tuileries. Moreover the scheme had long ago been anticipated by the pleasure-loving Parisians, this being one of the things that they order

better in France, as the witty Yorick
remarked.

CHARLES KEMBLE AND NAPOLEON III.

Kemble, rather deaf, spoke loudly; talking to Fladgate at the 'Garrick Club,
observing a gentleman standing before the
fire :

'Fladgate, who's that new man in the
hat ?'

'Allow the man in the hat to answer for
himself—I am Louis Napoleon, delighted
to hear Mr. Kemble's voice, on or off the
stage.'

ADELPHI 'JERRY.'

Yates detested dogs, and forbade any of
the canine tribe to be brought into the
theatre.   This ukase against the ladies'
pets produced consternation among the
theatrical sisterhood.   During a rehearsal
a roguish-looking cur, a sort of mongrel
terrier, found his way on the stage.

Tableau of horror! Yates speedily kicked him out, nothing afeard. He came again the next day, and despite of kicks and cuffs continued his visits daily, to the intense delight of the ladies. Our manager gave up the contest, vowing it was a 'dog fiend.' Jerry, so christened by our call-boy, had an ear for music—always sat near the big drum, appearing to be delighted by the sound, frisking and barking during the dancing (ballet). Jerry jumped, rolled, etc., trying to bite the ladies' feet. A dress rehearsal being held, Jerry was strictly prohibited from entering. No avail : there he was, covered with mud, by his favourite drum. Yates, enraged, ordered him to be tied to the prompt-table, fearing he would spoil the dresses. Music commenced, big drum, very loud in certain passages. This was too much for poor Jerry—away he dashed, dragging table, books, ink, upsetting the prompter, knocking down Yates, before he reached his beloved drum! Universal uproar, laughter, screams, curses, and broomsticks, drove Jerry out at the stage-door. He never returned. Some weeks after this he was seen in St. James's Park following the band, walking close to the big drum. Hailed by his friend the call-boy, Jerry wagged his tail and marched on.

YATES DYING.

Yates, dying, complained to a friend that he had been refused an order by the managers of Drury Lane.

'That was unkind,' said his friend, 'to an old servant.'

'Yes; when my admission could not have kept a living soul out of the house. I only wanted their order to let me be buried under the stage.'

PUNCH'S PANTOMIME, 1842.

'Punch's Pantomime, or Harlequin King John and Magna Charta,' produced and written by the writers of *Punch*—Mark Lemon, Gilbert A'Beckett, Tom Hood, Albert Smith, Douglas Jerrold, etc.—performed at the Theatre Royal, Covent Garden (under Madame Vestris's management), on Boxing-night, 1842. Despite the talented concoctors, authors, etc., of this Christmas offering to the public, a signal failure attended it. Those that saw 'Punch' on the stage came away disappointed. 'Too many cooks spoil the broth,' so runs the adage, verified in this case. 'Punch' proved unsavoury and unprofitable.

ORIGINAL CAST AND BILL OF 'PUNCH'S PANTOMIME.'

OBERON (a mere wreck of the Rex of the Fairies), *Miss Kendall.*

TITANIA (a Queen to match), *Mrs. Emden.*

PUCK (mischief-maker to the Court by appointment), *Miss James.*

PUNCH (the peripatetic), *Miss Taylor.*

PEA-BLOSSOM, *Miss Hunt.*

MOTH, *Miss Partridge.*

CODWEB, *Miss A. Payne.*

MUSTARD-SEED, *Miss A. Hunt.*

KING JOHN (a character naturally drawn by Shakespeare, now a little over-drawn by Punch), *Mr. W. H. Payne.*

COUNT LA MARCHE (a Conjugal Paradox, who evidently didn't know his own interests, being angry with the man who stole his wife), *Mr. J. Ridgway.*

BARON FITZWALTER (editor of 'Magna Charta' and other 'Popular Information for the People'), *Mr. S. Smith.*

AARON LEVI (a Jew, standing in the relation of uncle to most of the Barons), *Mr. T. Ireland.*

HUBERT (the King's table-decker and odd man, with touch of human nature, according to Hume and Smollett), *Mr. T. Ridgway.*

Lord Chancellor (generally wool-gathering), *Mr. Braithwaite.*

Chancellor of the Exchequer, *Mr. Gough.*

Baron de Audley, *Collett.*

Baron de Smith, *Butler.*

Baron de Jones, *Burt.*

Baron de Brown, *Connell.*

Baron de Robinson, *Melville.*

Baron de Nathan, *Hodge.*

Baron de Potts, *Sherwood.*

Baron de Roe, *Jones.*

Baron de Green, *Davis.*

Baron de Tims, *Sharpe.*

Baron de Gibs, *Gledhill.*

Baron de Jinks, *Macarthy.*

Baron de Dobbs, *Barker.*

Baron de White, *Healey.*

Baron de Phipps, *Guichard.*

Baron de Thoms, *Morgan.*

Musical Conductor, Warder, Messengers, Retainers, etc., etc.

44—2

AVISA (Queen No. 1, and late Countess la Marche), *Miss Garden.*

ISABELLA (Queen No. 2. on a separate maintenance), *Miss Moore.*

Fairies.

The overture and the whole of the music hetero- and in-geniously selected and composed by Mr. R. Hughes.

The scenery by T. and W. Grieve.

The mechanical changes, transmogrifications, and decorations, designed and executed by Mr. W. Bradwell.

The dresses (not after Stultz, but some considerable time before), by Miss Glover and Miss Rayner.

The multifarious machinery by Mr. H. Sloman.

The pantomime produced (with all the gorgeousness of the East) under the direction of Mr. W. West, junr.

ORATORIOS.

During Lent, at Drury Lane and Covent Garden, on given Wednesdays and Fridays, foreign vocalists and English musicians of reputation gave these sacred musical entertainments. A bold attempt to unite scenic and dramatic effects with music was made at Covent Garden, in ' Moses in Egypt.' Hebrews were seen passing through the Red Sea, singing hymns of praise ; Pharaoh and his host sinking beneath the waves. The Bishop of London remonstrated in the House of Lords ; and Moses was forbidden to cross the Red Sea for the future. Exeter Hall still gives these musical morceaux with fine bands and numerous choruses, led by Sir Michael Costa.

WILLIAM BEVERLEY.

This clever scenic artist is a worthy inheritor of the position in Old Drury once held by Clarkson Stanfield and David Roberts. The talents of this inventive man have been for many years confined scenically to Drury Lane. He it is who correctly and artistically illustrates the plays, pantomime openings, etc., that have created so much attention and won so much patronage in this temple of Thespis. Honest work ! no resorting to tricky, realistic effects, etc., in order to win momentary applause. Garish colours are eschewed by this true artist. Nature and nature's laws are strictly adhered to : meretricious devices scattered to the winds. Beverley lives at once to please the million and to satisfy connoisseurs.

> ' 26, Russell Square,
> 'Sept. 26, 1871.

' MY DEAR MR. STIRLING,

'I am truly sorry that you have found it necessary to withdraw from Drury Lane. At the same time, I think you have done the right thing. Without respect paid to the position you held, no business could go properly on. I am very glad you think we have worked comfortably together, for such was my intention, and I hope we shall soon meet again.

   ' With every kind wish,

      ' Believe me, yours sincerely,

            'W. R. BEVERLEY.

' E. Stirling, Esq.'

ANDERSON, THE WIZARD OF THE NORTH.

Covent Garden Theatre, built 1808, opened 1809, from designs of Sir R. Smirke, at a cost of £150,000, was totally destroyed by fire in 1856.* Lessee, the Wizard of the North—Anderson. This extraordinary man had travelled all over the known globe, seeking adventure and gold. A fatality attended his theatrical enterprises : every theatre that he rented

* The present Covent Garden was built by E. M. Barry.

was burnt—Glasgow, Liverpool, Covent Garden. Was this a conjuror's trick, or chance? a question still unanswered. Strange to relate, the destruction of his theatres never occurred in the pantomime season; always after. Suffice it, the Wizard tried many schemes of legerdemain, but it was out of fashion; rivals had exhibited 'sleight of hand' in a new style, 'without collusion.' The last time I saw Anderson was at the Railway Hotel, Liverpool, and the Claimant of the Tichborne estates was with him, hatching conjuring tricks for Westminster Hall. It is a curious coincidence that the Australian witness, Jean Luie, appeared on the scene a short time after this meeting at Liverpool. Aztec children, talking fish (*à la* Barnum), and acting Rob Roy, filled up our Wizard's leisure hours, quite apart from his nightly magic. Anderson died poor, as he commenced.

THE QUEEN AND THE VOCALIST.

Miss Louisa Pyne, shortly after commencing her management of Covent Garden in 1858, was engaged to sing at one of her Majesty's private concerts, at Buckingham Palace. The Queen and the Prince Consort complimented her on her singing; her Majesty kindly inquiring how her managerial speculation answered.

'Your Majesty, very well. "Lurline," a new opera by Wallace, is drawing good houses.'

The Queen seemed delighted to hear it, and responded:

'Miss Pyne, let it run; make all the money you can, and take care to keep it.'

Counsel convincing as any demonstration in mathematics.

THE PRINCE CONSORT AND THE FAIRY RIFLES AT COVENT GARDEN.

The threatened French invasion roused the British lion, male and female, to arm. Tennyson's 'Form, form! Riflemen, form!' helped the movement. Producing a pantomime at Covent Garden, with the aid of a drill-sergeant, I formed a fairy rifle corps of ladies, with silver rifles and beautiful uniform. The idea took well with the public. Her Majesty, the Prince Consort, and the Royal children came to see their manœuvring in the ballet scene—sixty pretty girls. After the performance, Harrison was sent for by the Prince, who told him how much her Majesty and himself were pleased.

'Little fear of invasion now, Mr. Harrison, with such defenders as your Fairy Corps. No soldiers in Europe could resist the fire of such riflemen's eyes.'

LORD LYTTON'S 'SEA-CAPTAIN.'

It was proposed to revive a play of Lord Lytton's, 'The Sea-Captain,' originally acted at the Haymarket, under Macready. Considerable alterations were to be made in the text by the author. He wrote to me on the subject :

> 'Buxton, Derbyshire,
>
> 'Sept. 12, 1868.
>
> 'DEAR SIR,
>
> 'My copy of the play has gone to the printer's. If not too great a trouble, can I ask you to let me have another, including the last corrections ?
>
> 'Yours,
>
> 'LYTTON.'

The play, rewritten, was produced under a new title as 'The Rightful Heir,' at the Lyceum Theatre, October 3, 1868.

A LETTER OF CHARLES DICKENS.

Charles Dickens, then giving his last readings at St. James's Hall, was urgently solicited by the ladies and gentlemen of the theatrical profession to give two or three morning readings, that they might have an opportunity of hearing him.   His reply was as follows :

> ' Gad's-hill-place,
> ' Higham by Rochester, Kent,
>   'Wednesday, March 24, 1869.

' LADIES AND GENTLEMEN,

' I beg to assure you that I am much gratified by the desire you do me the honour to express in your letter handed to me by Mr. John Clarke.

' Before that letter reached me I had heard of your wish, and had mentioned to Messrs. Chappell that it would be highly agreeable to me to anticipate it if possible.

They readily responded, and we agreed upon having three morning readings in London. As they are not yet publicly announced, I add a note of the days and subjects :

'Saturday, May 1st, "Boots at the Holly-Tree Inn," and "Sikes and Nancy," from "Oliver Twist."

'Saturday, May 8th, "The Christmas Carol."

'Saturday, May 22nd, "Sikes and Nancy," from "Oliver Twist," and "The Trial," from "Pickwick."

'With the warmest interest in your art, and in its claims upon the general gratitude and respect,

'Believe me always

'Faithfully your friend,

'CHARLES DICKENS.*

'To the ladies and gentlemen—my correspondents through Mr. Clarke.'

* See 'Letters of Charles Dickens,' vol. ii. pp. 418, 419.

MR. SOTHERN.

I asked 'Lord Dundreary' (Sothern) for his photograph. His lordship kindly complied with my request, and sent it with the following note :

'121, Harley-street, W.,

'July 16, 1871.

' DEAR STIRLING,

'Here you are, or rather here *I* am! There's a good deal of the melancholy nigger minstrel about it ; but it's the best I have. Your criticism is far too kind ; but all actors have a dash of vanity, and it's pleasant to have one's hair rubbed down the right way sometimes. Yes, I'm off to America in September, opening there on the 23rd October ; and, D.V., you'll see me back again in Old England about April next.

' Ever yours truly,

' E. A. SOTHERN.'

WILLIAM ALEXANDER.

William Alexander, proprietor of the Glasgow Theatre, a remarkable character, well known in Scotland for economy and for looking after the 'bawbees.' After many years' toil and penurious living he managed to purchase the ground in Dunlop-street, Glasgow, and build a fine theatre. This building of stone was graced with statues of Shakespeare, Milton, Scott, Byron, etc. ; above all (perhaps with pardonable vanity) William Alexander. Declining years brought retirement to the canny Scot ; but his savings were unfortunately invested in the Western Bank of Scotland, and after his death a sad event occurred—its failure ! which to his widow brought poverty. Alexander being taken ill in London, was induced, after much persuasion, to send for a celebrated physician. When Sir William

Forbes saw him, he told him to prepare for death, his case being hopeless. Poor Alexander, starting wildly up in his bed,

' Ye dunna mean to say that I am to die, doctor ?'

FORBES: ' I fear there is no chance of your recovery, Mr. Alexander.'

'What! after all my working and striving for forty years, not live—not live to enjoy it ?' (*with a deep groan*) ; ' then it's a cursed shame.'

Few persons know how to be old.

E. L. BLANCHARD.

Drury's comic poet and pantomimic historian of fairy lore, Lord of Misrule, children's master of Christmas revels. This cheery, amiable man seems ever green. No clouds beset E. L. Blanchard, without silver lining. He is the son of a worthy sire, an excellent actor of character and old men's parts at Covent Garden, under the Kemble *régime*. He is an impartial critic in the *Era* and the *Daily Telegraph*, the author of useful and interesting works ; but more essentially is he the friend of children—author and concoctor of their Christmas wonders. What would Christmas holidays be, or Christmas pudding, without Blanchard's racy bill of fare at Old Drury ?

HOW TO WRITE AN ORIGINAL ENGLISH PLAY.

Let a regular dramatic cook take two French pieces, strip them of their idioms, mix them well up together, spiced with a few jokes from Mr. Joseph Miller, no matter how often they have been used ; throw in English names by way of seasoning. When the whole is properly dressed, send the MS. to a manager. Served up in a proper theatre, with the aid of good actors, the piece goes down as a genuine English composition (a recipe from the famous Dr. Kitchener).

THE DUKES OF BEDFORD AND THE TWO GREAT THEATRES.

Dukes of Bedford, ground landlords of Drury Lane and Covent Garden Theatres. This fortunate family are indebted largely to their wise and politic ancestor, Sir W. Russell, a prime favourite of Henry VIII. Russell, one of the pious King's executors and commissioner of sequestrated Church property, had a goodly share in the whole-sale plunder of monasteries, convents, and monkish establishments.   Henry's Royal grants, Woburn Abbey, Tavistock Priory, the Convent lands (hence at this day Covent[*] Garden Market and Theatre), Drury Lane, were all wrested from the Catholic Church, and are now of immense value.   When we reflect that previous to this spoliation the poor, the aged, and the destitute were supported by monastic estab-lishments, dole-giving at every gate with

* A corruption of *Convent.*

unsparing hand—there were no poor's rates or workhouses before Elizabeth's reign of glorious memory—the change does not seem altogether for the better. The motto of the illustrious house of Bedford indicates their belief in their own rights. ' Che sarà sarà '—Whatever is, is right.

CURIOUS OLD PLAYS, ETC.,
1512—1774.

'CANDLEMAS DAY, OR THE KILLING OF THE CHILDREN OF ISRAEL,' 1512.

'A Mysterie.' In this old play the Hebrew soldiers swear by Mahomet, who was not born till 600 years after; Herod's messenger is named ' Watkin,' and the knights are directed to walk about the stage, while Mary and the infant are conveyed to Egypt.

FIRST REGULARLY CONSTRUCTED PLAY

(the scene laid in London) is called ' Ralph Royster Doyster.' It was produced in the reign of Henry VIII. It is in five acts and thirteen scenes.

'JACOB AND ESAU,'

An Interlude, 1568. This is a very early piece, written in metre, and printed in old black-letter. Its full title runs thus: 'A new, merry, and witty Comedie or Enterlude newlie imprinted, treating upon the Historie of Jacob and Esau, taken out of the 27th chapter of the first book of Moses, entitled Genesis.' In the title-page are the parts and names of the players, who are to be considered Hebrews, 'and so should be apparailed with attire.'

'THE FOUR P'S,'

A merry Interlude of a Palmer, a Pardoner, a 'Potycary, and a Pedlar, by John Fleetwood, 1569. This is one of the first plays that appeared in the English language; it is written in metre, and is not divided into acts.

'APPIUS AND VIRGINIA,'

A tragedy by R. P., 1576, in black-letter, and not divided into acts, 'where in' (as it is set forth in the title-page) 'is lively expressed a rare example of the vertue of chastity in wishing rather to be slaine at her owne Fathers hands then to become a victim of the wicked Judge Appius.' This old play is evidently the source of Sheridan Knowles's 'Virginius,' performed originally at Glasgow, and reproduced at Drury Lane by Macready. Virginius was one of Macready's best personations. It always commanded good houses, and gave universal satisfaction.

'THE SCHOOL OF ABUSE.'

A book entitled 'The School of Abuse,' written by Stephen Gosson, 1579. A pleasant abuse against poets, pipers, players, jesters, and such like caterpillars of the Commonwealth, dedicated to Sir Philip Sidney.

AN OLD PLAY.

An old play, called ' The Pleasant and Stately Morall of the Three Lords and Three Ladies of London,' 1590, written by one Paul Bucke (whose name is subscribed at the end, 'Finis—Paul Bucke),' is a curious tribute to the memory of Tarlton, Queen Elizabeth's jester and Shakespearian clown, who died only a short time before. Simplicity, a clown, a sort of inferior Autolycus, enters with a basket, singing ballads ; afterwards a countryman takes what is called a picture ' of Tarlton ' out of the basket, and asks who it is.   Simplicity pronounces an eulogium upon him, ending thus :

' But it was the merriest fellow that had such jests in
     store,
   That if thou hadst seen him, thou wouldst have
     laughed thy heart sore.'

'A WARNING FOR FAIR WOMEN.'

Tragedy, 1590.   This old play was greatly in vogue in Queen Elizabeth's time.

The plot was founded on facts, viz.—'the most lamentable and tragical murder of Mr. George Saunders, of London, at Shooter's Hill—the crime consented unto by his own wife, assisted by Captain George Brown, Mrs. Dury, and Trusty Roger, agents therein, with their several ends at Tyburn Tree.'   This play is printed in black-letter ; the above is a transcript of the title-page.

'DAVID AND BETHSABE,'

Their loves and consequences, with the tragedy of Absalom's death, divers times played on the stage with musick, 1599.   The title of this play speaks for itself.   It was several times acted with applause at the Cock-pit in Drury Lane.*

'SIR GYLES GOOSE,'

A comedy, 1606.   This play was first acted by the children of the Chapel Royal, with great applause.   It was afterwards

* The Cock-pit was the site of Drury Lane Theatre.

presented at a private house in Salisbury-court, and finally at Lincoln's Inn Fields Theatre.

'LINGUA.'

'Lingua, or the Combat of the Tongue and the Five Senses for superiority,' a serious comedy (author unknown), 1607. At the first performance of it at Trinity College, Cambridge, Oliver Cromwell, then a scholar, acted the part of Tacitus in it. The scene is laid in a grove—Microcosmus. Time, from morning till night.

'THE SHOEMAKERS HOLIDAY, OR THE GENTLE CRAFT',

'With the humours of Simson Eyre, shoemaker and Lord Mayor of London.' A comedy, 1610. It is dedicated to all good fellows, professors of the gentle craft, of what degree soever. It is printed in black-letter, and not divided into acts.

'THE MASQUE OF FLOWERS,' 1614.

This Masque was presented by gentlemen of Gray's Inn, at the Court at Whitehall, in the Banqueting-house, upon Twelfth Night, 1613, and was one of the solemnities and magnificences which were performed at the marriage of the Earl of Somerset, the favourite of James I. (the suspected poisoner of Sir Edmund Godfrey).

'CUPID'S WHIRLIGIG,'

A Comedy, 1616. Coxeter relates that this play was entered at Westminster Hall as Shakespeare's, but at that time thought falsely, in order to make it sell. A lie has short legs.

'ANYTHING FOR A QUIET LIFE,'

A Comedy, by T. Middleton. Acted at Blackfriars, 1625. The plot of this play is a game at Chess, played between the Church of England and the Church of Rome, wherein the former comes off victorious; Ignatius Loyola, the Jesuit, being a spectator. This play was in much

esteem before the breaking out of the Civil
Wars.

'THE NEW INN, OR LIGHT HEART,'

A Comedy, by Ben Jonson, 1631. It did
not succeed, according to the author's idea.
He published on the title-page this tirade:
'" The New Inn, or the Light Heart," a
Comedy, never acted, but most shamefully
played by some of the King's men
(servants), and more squeamishly censured
by others the King's subjects, 1629, now
at last set at liberty to the readers to be
judged by themselves.'

'WHEN YOU SEE ME, YOU KNOW ME;

'Or, the famous Chronicle History of King
Henry VIII., with the birth and virtuous
life of Edward, Prince of Wales,' by Sam.
Rowley, 1632. The plot of this piece is
taken from Lord Herbert's 'Life of Henry
VIII.,' and other English historians. The
scene lies in England.

'CRUELTY OF THE SPANIARDS.'

Oliver Cromwell (1658) at the play, Cock-pit, Drury-lane, to see a piece called ' The Cruelty of the Spaniards in Peru,' expressed by instrumental and vocal music, and by the art of perspective scenery ; represented daily at the Cock-pit, in Drury-lane, at three in the afternoon, punctually. Cromwell, who had prohibited all theatrical representations, not only allowed this piece to be performed, but even himself read and approved of it. The reason assigned for this was that it strongly reflected on the Spaniards, against whom he had formed some considerable state design.

'THE BIRTH OF MERLIN,'

A tragi-comedy, by W. Rowley. The scene lies in Britain ; the story is taken from Geoffrey of Monmouth. Shakespeare was once believed to have assisted in writing this play, and his name is on the title-page of the edition published in 1662.

'THE WARY WIDOW,'

A comedy, produced at Drury Lane, 1693, was damned the first night, through a curious circumstance. The author, in a drinking scene, gave the actors too much punch. They were all intoxicated, and totally unable to speak their parts. The audience, enraged, hissed and pelted them. The house was dismissed at the end of the third act.—*Old Newspaper*, 1693.

'THREE HOURS AFTER MARRIAGE,'

A farce in three acts, written by Pope, Gay, and Arbuthnot, in 1717. This little piece, the joint production of a triumvirate of first-rate wits, was acted at the Theatre Royal, Drury Lane, and deservedly damned. From this *contretemps* Pope conceived such a disgust to the stage, that he never attempted to write for it again.

'LOVE IS A RIDDLE.'

Pastoral opera, Drury Lane, 1728. Written by Cibber, in imitation of the 'Beggar's Opera:' it came out in the succeeding year, and met with a most severe and unjust reception, causing a general disturbance in all parts of the house, excepting when Miss Rastor (Mrs. Clive) was singing. She made her first appearance in it, and Frederick, Prince of Wales, the son of George II., was present for the first time after his arrival in these kingdoms.

Mr. Cibber came forward and assured the audience, that if they would suffer the performance to go on quietly for that night, out of respect to the Royal presence, the piece should not be acted any more; and he kept his word.

'PERSEUS.'

There are two dramatic pieces of this name: the first was performed at Drury

Lane, 1728; the other at Lincoln's Inn
Fields, 1730. One of them appears to
have been outrageously indecent, and is
severely commented on in the *Grub-street
Journal*, April 8th, 1731. Its title is
' Perseus and Andromeda, with the Rape
of Columbine, or the Flying Lovers,' in
five interludes—three serious, two comic.
The serious composed by Monsieur Roger,
the comic by John Weaver, dancing-
master.

The following was printed in the *Grub-
street Journal :*

' It should be known by posterity, that in
the year 1730, the simplicity and innocence
of our women were at such a pitch, that
they could appear for three-score nights
together at an immoral entertainment, in
which the most lascivious acts were repeatedly represented, and of which they
were so entirely ignorant and unexperi-
enced, that they could not guess what it

meant, nor were so much as put to the expense of a blush.'

'LILLIPUT,'

A musical entertainment, 1757. This piece was acted by children ; there was no great amount of merit in it. It was performed at Drury Lane for Woodward's benefit, as a novelty. There is nothing new, however, under the sun ; we were led to believe that children's pantomimes, operas, and acting, were novelties in our days.

'ART OF MANAGEMENT, OR TRAGEDY EXPELLED,'

A dramatic piece, by Mrs. Charlotte Charke (a younger daughter of Colley Cibber), was performed once at the Concert-room in York Buildings. This piece was intended as a satire on Charles Fleetwood, then manager of Drury Lane Theatre ; but that gentleman and his party found means to put a stop to its further progress on the stage. It was printed in 1735. with a humorous dedication to Mr. Fleetwood, who endeavoured to smother it by purchasing the whole impression. Some few copies escaped the flames, and have crept into the world.

FIRST MELODRAMA EVER ACTED ON THE ENGLISH STAGE.

'TALE OF MYSTERY,'

Adapted from the French, written by an actor, called 'Seline, or the Maid of Savoy. (Holcroft introduced the piece.) The original cast was as follows :

COVENT GARDEN, NOVEMBER, 1760.

ROMALDI, *Henry Johnston.*
FRANCISCO, *Farley.*
BORNAMO, *Murray.*
STEPHANO, *Brunton.*
FIAMETTA, *Mrs. Mattocks.*
LOUISE, *Mrs. Gibbs.*

Malvoglio, *Cory.*
The Miller, *Blanchard.*
Montano, *Claremont.*

'THE WISHES, OR HARLEQUIN'S MOUTH OPENED,'

A comedy by Bentley, 1761, brought on the stage at Drury Lane, last summer, by the company under the management of Messrs. Foote and Murphy. It is written in imitation of the Italian comedy, Harlequin, Pantaloon, Pierrot, Mezzetin, Colombine, being introduced into it, as speaking characters. The oddity of a set of characters which the English audience had been accustomed to see only in the light of mute mimics, was relished mightily. It is said a Great Personage had some hand in this composition of wit and just satire on the manners of the day. The King sent the author a handsome present.'—*Daily Courant*, 1761.

'ACCOMPLISHED MAID.'

'Accomplished Maid,' Drury Lane, 1766, December 4th. A translation from the celebrated Italian opera of Goldoni, called ' La Buona Figliuola.' This was the first attempt at bringing an entire Italian musical composition on the English stage, by applying our language to the harmony of theirs. Bickerstaff's ' Maid of the Mill' owes its origin to the same story of Goldoni.

'BETTY, OR THE COUNTRY BUMPKIN,'

A ballad opera, by Harry Carey, Edmund Kean's grandfather on the mother's side. The piece failed signally at Drury Lane on the first night.

'THE GOLDEN RUMP.'

This piece was never acted, nor was it

ever known who was the author; yet it caused a remarkable event in dramatic history, whereby all pieces are obliged to undergo the inspection and censure of the Lord Chamberlain, before they can be represented. This piece was offered to Henry Giffard, the manager of Goodman's Fields Theatre, for representation. With a most unbounded freedom, abuse was directed in it against Parliament, the Privy Council, the Ministry, and the King. Giffard, like an honest manager and a loyal subject, carried the piece to the Home Secretary, to consult him on the matter. The Minister received the MS., and at the same time, that he (Giffard) might be no loser by his zeal for his King and country, he ordered a sum of money equal to what he reasonably might have expected from the 'Golden Rump' performances, to be paid to him. This caused a Bill to be immediately passed through Parliament to control all stage productions by a Lord Chamberlain's supervision (1774).

INDEX.

THE END.

9 783741 168062